Family Secrets

by

Debra St. John

Family Secrets

Cover Art by *Angela Anderson*

The Wild Rose Press, Inc.
PO Box 708
Adams Basin, NY 14410-0708
Visit us at www.thewildrosepress.com

Publishing History
First Champagne Rose Edition, 2014
Print ISBN 978-1-62830-433-6
Digital ISBN 978-1-62830-434-3

She shook off the feeling, and once again attempted to concentrate on the movie. Soon the girls drifted off and, eager for something to do to keep her mind off forbidden topics, she rose to gather the remains of their snack. She reached for the empty popcorn bowl as Chase did the same. Her hand brushed his, and she yanked it away as if burned.

"Erika." Her name came out soft. Husky. Never before had it sounded so intimate on a man's lips.

"I need to get this cleaned up." She fled to the kitchen.

She stood by the sink, the snack dishes forgotten. Her hands gripped the edge of the granite so hard her knuckles turned white.

The soft pad of Chase's bare feet announced his arrival a moment before his hands came to rest on her shoulders. She flinched.

"Erika." How easily she could get used to him saying her name just like that. As though velvet secrets hid in the simple syllables. She shivered under his touch. "What are you thinking?"

As if he didn't know. She shook her head, unable to speak, or unwilling to voice her thoughts aloud.

With gentle hands he turned her to face him. "Look at me." He lifted her chin with a finger.

She tried to tear her gaze from his, but the intensity in the dark depths of his eyes made the task impossible. The silent communication spoke to her soul in a way nothing ever had before.

Dedication

To John...thanks for being my love, my life, my family,
my everything.

And to our families,
whose love, support, and encouragement
never fail to honor and humble me.
(So, don't worry, I didn't spill any of our secrets!)

Chapter One

"Why didn't you call me?"

The bold words took Erika Garrett by surprise. But no more so than the man standing on her doorstep who had uttered them. She gazed up at him. An errant lock of dark hair fell over one eyebrow, daring her to reach up and brush it back. His chiseled features bore a dark, even tan, evidence of his outside work in the summer. A hint of stubble shadowed his jaw and made him look sexy as hell. Warm brown eyes crinkled at the corners when he smiled.

Chase Stewart was as gorgeous as ever.

"Hello, Erika." Once again the deep timbre of his familiar voice washed over her, and she stared, caught up in the penetrating gaze of the man who evoked such powerful memories.

"Chase. What are you doing here?" She couldn't remember the last time she'd seen him. What was he doing on her doorstep?

Instead of answering the question, he asked one of his own. "It's hot as blazes out here today. May I come in?"

She hesitated. But then, as if to underscore his words, a blast of hot air hit her like the heat from an open oven. The scorching afternoon sun poured into the house. Nothing like a Midwest summer to make you feel like a fried egg. It had been so hot this year the evening news had done a story on kids literally frying them on the sidewalk. And it was only June.

"Well, I guess there's no use cooling the outside." The air conditioning bill would be high enough anyway. She stepped back and opened the door wider.

Chase stood in the foyer of the historic row home and studied her as she closed the door. "You look terrific."

"Thanks." She self-consciously touched the curling locks she'd pinned to the top of her head in an effort to control the humidity's effect on them. She adjusted the slim strap of her tank top, and then smoothed her palms over her shorts.

He looked terrific, too. No surprise there. Had she always been turned on by men in jeans and work boots? Not to mention white T-shirts that drew attention to the muscles beneath. A blush warmed her cheeks and she looked away. Had he noticed her staring?

"So this is your new place."

She glanced back at him to find his gaze had moved to the living room behind her. Two beige sofas faced each other in the middle of the narrow room. A coffee table sat between them, resting on a colorfully patterned rug. Centered on the side wall, built-in book shelves and stained glass windows framed the fireplace. Past the stairs a narrow hallway led to the kitchen.

What did it look like through his eyes? Professional eyes. What did he see? Would he notice the fading paint and battered woodwork?

She shrugged. "It's home."

"It's nice."

Unable to hold his mesmerizing gaze, hers dropped to her toes. The scuffed hardwood of the floor stared back at her. "It, uh, needs a little work, but it's getting there." She planned on doing some of the interior painting during vacation.

"That's why I'm here."

Her head jerked up. "What?"

"I heard you need some things done around here."

"How did you hear that?" Surely Lauren hadn't said anything. She barely spoke civilly to Chase. Erika couldn't imagine the topic of home repair—*her* home repair—coming up.

"Not many people around here do what I do. It's a small world. A buddy mentioned he gave you a quote." His dark eyes bored into hers once again. "So, why didn't you call me?"

"I thought it would be awkward, with my family and all."

"The family?"

"You know, Mom and Lauren…" Her voice trailed off.

"What about them?"

"Oh come on, Chase." He couldn't really be so obtuse, could he? "They would have a fit if they knew you were here. Can you imagine what they would say if I hired you?"

"That's ridiculous. Why would they care?"

Did she have to spell it out? "You know how Lauren is." She didn't want to speak badly about her sister-in-law, but the other woman didn't have many good things to say about her ex-husband these days. Or ever. If Lauren found out he'd been at Erika's place…

"Oh, I know how Lauren is," Chase said wryly. "But this has nothing to do with her. This isn't about her. It's about me helping you."

Erika shook her head. "I don't—"

"Why don't we discuss this over a glass of lemonade?"

"What?" Her head spun from the abrupt change in topic.

"Offer me a glass of lemonade, and we can talk about this rationally. I assume the kitchen's through here?" Without waiting for a reply, he headed down the hallway.

She stared after him, her mouth open. With a disgruntled sigh, she followed. In the kitchen Chase flipped one of the ladder-back chairs around and straddled the seat, as if he were accustomed to making himself at home in her house. But then again, why shouldn't he? After all, he was family. Sort of.

The conundrum of their relationship made her head spin. Erika put her hands on her hips. "What makes you think I have lemonade?"

He grinned. "You always have lemonade in the summer." His expression sobered. "I know you, Erika."

She turned away. The bottles in the door of the refrigerator rattled as she opened it with more force than necessary. Chase did know her. Perhaps better than anyone. He'd been there for her at a time when she really needed someone. But all that had happened in the past, and it was best if it stayed there. No good would come from dredging it up.

She retrieved tall glasses from the cabinet next to the sink. Her hand trembled as she filled them and drops of lemonade splashed onto the counter. Not wanting it to get sticky, she wiped the spill, and then returned the pitcher to the fridge. The ice cubes in the glasses clinked as she set the beverages on the table nestled in a bay-windowed alcove facing the backyard. She sat across from Chase.

He swallowed a large gulp. His adam's apple bobbed in his throat. The masculine feature enthralled her. The glass looked fragile and small in his strong, sure hands. She remembered how comforting those hands could be.

She shook her head to clear the disturbing memory. She nibbled on the nail of her left thumb. "So, how have you been?" Lauren never mentioned him unless she was griping about something. Although Erika would never admit it to her family, she missed him at their gatherings.

His warm, brown eyes met hers. "I'm doing okay. How about you?"

"About the same." She traced a finger through the condensation on her glass. "Getting used to the way things are now."

He nodded.

She changed the subject. "At Mom's house the other day Sami and Steph were talking about going to kindergarten in the fall."

His eyes softened at the mention of his twin four-year-olds. "I can't believe how fast they're growing."

She smiled. "It seems like just yesterday you were bringing them home from the hospital."

"Tell me about it."

"How are the custody arrangements working out for you?"

He grimaced. "I miss seeing them every day. Tucking them into bed each night. When I pick them up on the weekends, I feel like I've missed out on so much during the week." His expression turned thoughtful.

"Funny, isn't it?"

"What?"

"Well, you know how I felt when Lauren told me she was pregnant?"

He hadn't been overjoyed, if memory served right.

"I wasn't ready to be a father. Hell, I never planned on being a husband, let alone a dad. But now, I can't imagine my life without my girls. They're the most important thing in the world to me. I never thought I could love anybody the way I love those girls."

Erika's heart constricted with sympathy. Chase adored his girls, and the divorce had limited his time with them. But his words triggered other feelings. His dedication to his daughters and how he loved them so desperately made her almost jealous. What would it feel like to be the object of such single-minded devotion?

"Anyway." He shook his head as if shaking off the melancholy thoughts. "Come winter I should be able to spend more time with them. But my schedule doesn't permit it right now." He gazed at her again. "And speaking of, I need to fit you into it."

She shook her head. "Chase, really, I don't think that's a good idea. I—"

"What all needs to be done?" He glanced around. "This room looks like it's been remodeled recently."

"About a year ago." The kitchen, with its stainless steel appliances, dark stained oak cabinets, and granite counters, wasn't on the list of things to do. None of which were Chase's concern. She folded her arms across her chest and glared at him. "Are you listening to me?"

"Humor me a minute and tell me what needs to be done."

She huffed out a sigh. He'd always been stubborn. "The front porch needs to be rebuilt, the outside trim needs to be painted, and a bunch of windows need to be replaced."

"Okay." He pushed back his chair. The castors slid smoothly across the hardwood floor. "Let's go take a look."

She opened her mouth to protest, but he'd already headed toward the front door. When she caught up with him outside, he had pencil and paper in hand and was making notes.

The sticky humidity was suffocating. The thick air enveloped her in its clinging shroud. Half a dozen pots on the porch held wilting and straggly petunias. No matter how often she watered them, they were losing the battle to the oppressive heat. "Ugh. It's hot today."

"It's summer in Chicago, what do you expect?"

"Well, I didn't expect to be out here arguing with you. Seriously, I have this under control."

He ignored her. "I'll probably subcontract the painting out, but the rest I'll handle myself."

She groaned and put her hands on her hips. "Are you deaf? Or are you purposely trying to irritate me to death? I can't hire you."

"Can't? Or won't?"

She lowered her gaze. He still could read her well. "Does it matter? Besides," she rushed on before he could interrupt again. "I already have a couple of estimates, and I'm going to use one of those contractors. The price is fair, and he can get the job done in my time frame."

"What's your time frame?"

She told him.

He whistled. "Why so soon?"

"I got a really good deal on this place. A really good deal. But there were conditions. Getting the repairs done on the outside is one of them. And everything needs to be historically accurate, yet up to current code. If I don't have the repairs done by the deadline, or if I'm in violation of code, I'll be fined by the village."

"What were the other estimates?"

"I can't tell you that."

"Of course you can, don't be ridiculous."

She sighed. "I don't remember off the top of my head, but I'm going to go with the lowest one. And that's final."

"I wish I could do it all for you for free, but I can't."

The kind gesture sidetracked her from her adamant refusal. "I'd never expect you to do that."

"I know, but I want you to know I would if I could afford it. However, I can guarantee I'll be the lowest bid. Remember, with me you're still eligible for the family discount."

"Don't you see? That's just it. It will be too complicated."

"No, it won't," he said. "Unless you make it that way."

"You're not taking *no* for an answer, are you?" She wiped the back of her hand across her moist forehead. It was too hot to be standing in the heat arguing.

"No." He smiled. "Erika, let me help you. I want to help you. Please."

She wavered at the earnest plea in his voice.

As if sensing her indecision, he added, "Tell you

what. Let me draw up a proposal. If someone else comes in with a lower bid, you can take that one if you'd rather."

A bead of sweat trickled down her spine. Time for the conversation to be over. If she stayed outside for much longer, she might ooze into a big puddle at his feet. "Fine. Draw up a proposal. *If* you're the lowest bid, I'll consider letting you do the job. But only if you're the lowest bid." Based on the numbers she already had, making the allowance shouldn't be a problem. No way could Chase underbid the other contractor.

"Thank you." He glanced at his watch. "I have to get going. I have another estimate this afternoon."

"Do you have time for one more glass of lemonade before you hit the road?" The invitation slipped out. Despite her misgivings about him being there, and his insistence about working for her, it really had been good to see him. It seemed like forever since they'd chatted. She missed their long talks.

"Sure. That sounds great."

She opened the door, and he followed her back inside. The cool relief of the air conditioning reminded her how grateful she was the furnace hadn't needed replacing when she moved in. She gestured toward the living room. "Have a seat. I'll bring it out here."

When she returned from the kitchen, she found him not sitting on the couch, but staring at the wedding picture she still kept in a frame on the mantel. His gaze searched out and found hers.

"How are you really doing?"

The soft words sent her spinning back into the past, but she handed him his beverage before sitting on the sofa. "I'm fine. Really. Things took a bit of adjusting, but I'm okay now."

Chase set his glass on a coaster on the coffee table. He sat on the other couch across from her. He didn't respond, but looked at her with compassionate eyes.

"It's different, of course," she said at last. Her glance slipped to the framed photograph once again. "Sometimes I find myself waiting for Kevin to call and tell me he's going to be late, and then I remember..."

Silence fell. Comfortable. Companionable. It had always been easy between them.

"I'm proud of you," he said after a while.

The comment surprised her. "For what?"

"Look around. You've come a long way in the past year. This really is a nice place." He nodded to encompass the house.

"It's a great neighborhood, too. I can walk to the library and the bank and the coffee shop. The village is big enough to have enough amenities, but it also has a small-town feel. Everyone is really friendly."

"I'm glad you didn't stay in your old place."

"I wanted something of my own. Something without all the memories." She forced a rueful laugh. "I like being on my own and doing things for myself. And I make me a priority," she added, almost as an after thought.

"Which is something Kevin never did." His tone was neutral, but his eyes sparked with some undefined emotion.

"Kevin was a good man, and he loved me." The defense came automatically to her lips. Would Chase hear the lie in her words? "But he was...dedicated to his...job." Her voice faltered.

Chase started to say something, but stopped as if he'd changed his mind. "You're so strong," he said instead.

"You of all people know that's not true."

He didn't pretend to misunderstand. "Your husband had just died in a car accident, Erika. I think you were entitled to a crying jag." He reached across the coffee table and covered her hand with his own.

Her flesh immediately warmed beneath his, and she fought the urge to pull away. His touch meant to comfort, but her heart stuttered at the contact. Warmth, having nothing to do with the summer heat, flushed her body.

What was wrong with her? They'd been talking about her husband. Why did Chase's innocent gesture evoke a yearning ache within her?

Unsettled, she pulled away, but not before she glanced up and met his probing gaze. She wanted to lower her lids, afraid her thoughts would be visible in her eyes, but the answering heat in his froze her. She shivered.

She hugged herself. "You, uh, you probably should get going to that other estimate."

"Right." His voice sounded odd.

She walked him to the door, and then opened it to admit a gust of hot, humid air. "How do you work outside in this stuff?" Weather. A nice, safe topic.

He shrugged and grinned his killer smile. "You get used to it." He turned on the doorstep. "I'll have that estimate for you tomorrow. Promise you won't make a decision until you've seen my numbers."

She ignored the request. "Say hi to the girls for me."

11

"Will do." He leaned in and brushed a soft kiss across her cheek. The woodsy scent of his aftershave drifted over her. "Thanks for the talk, it's been a while."

"Yeah, it has."

He whistled on his way down the front brick walk toward his truck. The pickup roared to life at the curb. She waved when he honked, then shut the door, and leaned wearily against it for a minute.

Lauren would have a fit if she found out Chase had been there today. She couldn't even imagine what her mother-in-law's reaction would be. Erika pushed away from the door, a grim smile on her lips. Neither woman had good things to say about Chase.

Which meant Erika couldn't hire him. The enigmatic nature of their relationship didn't allow it.

What a shame. She'd seen his work. He had an impeccable reputation as an excellent carpenter. And what if by chance he did come in with the lowest bid? Although she wasn't looking for charity, he'd give her a fair price. On her limited budget, that rated a big plus.

It wouldn't have anything to do with his so-called family discount. His honesty and integrity were two of the many things she admired about him.

She plopped down on the loveseat and stared at the photograph above the fireplace. She and Kevin had started dating in college. Getting married had been a natural progression. But being married to Kevin hadn't been anything like she thought marriage would be. It hadn't been perfect. Far from it. Right before his death, he'd been away more than he'd been home, occupied with other things. Other women. If he hadn't been killed, would their marriage have ended in divorce? It had seemed to be heading there. Apparently neither of the Garrett siblings was good at making a marriage work.

Would she ever have the kind of marriage she dreamed about? Was it too late for her? She'd been a young bride, and now at twenty-eight, a young widow.

Then again, most people nowadays switched boyfriends like she switched coffee grounds. If she ever did get married again, she wanted a passionate, last-forever kind of love. And someone who made her the most important thing in his life. She'd never settle for being second best again.

****

Chase hummed tunelessly to the Johnny Cash song on the classic country radio station as he drove away from Erika's house. A smile tilted the corners of his mouth. It had been good to see her.

He hadn't lied when he told her she looked terrific. The wisps of light brown hair escaping the clip on top of her head had curled beguilingly around her face. And he'd had trouble keeping his eyes off the long, slender legs revealed by her shorts. Her wide eyes, so blue they rivaled the most perfect summer sky, lingered in his mind.

He groaned at the sappy poetic musings. He sounded like a freaking greeting card. Not to mention he shouldn't be thinking about Erika that way. She'd been widowed less than a year ago. And worse, her status as his ex-wife's sister-in-law, made those thoughts even more inappropriate.

Regardless, it had been great to talk to her. He missed their talks. Since his divorce, hell long before then, he hadn't exactly been on the top of the guest list for family gatherings. The girls were the only reason he stayed in contact with Lauren's family at all.

For Erika it was different. Even though Kevin was gone, she was still very much part of the family. She needed them. They needed her.

As in-laws, he and Erika had shared a certain camaraderie. It hadn't always been easy to fit into a very close-knit family. She'd done a hell of a better job than he had. He hadn't cared as much. She wanted to be part of a family like the Garretts. Even Kevin's death couldn't sever the ties binding her to his parents and sister.

Chase frowned. If she remained so attached to Kevin's family, would she ever move on with her life? Did she even want to?

Kevin's unexpected death had devastated her. The tears streaking down her cheeks and the empty, haunted look in her eyes the night of the funeral were etched into his memory. He'd never forgotten the agonized look on her face.

He hoped eventually she would be ready to move on. She had her whole life ahead of her. If she could only get over Kevin.

Not to speak ill of the dead, but Kevin didn't deserve her ongoing grief. He'd never been worthy of her. He never treated her the way she deserved.

At least she'd moved out of the house they'd shared. It was a good start toward beginning a new life for herself. The historic row house she'd bought seemed to be structurally sound, as far as he'd been able to tell from his very cursory inspection, but it needed a lot of minor repairs and cosmetic work. He wanted to do what he could to help. Maybe he could ease some of the pain still lingering in her eyes.

If she let him. Had she always been so stubborn? Why didn't she want his help? She'd been adamant about only accepting the lowest bid.

Well, he'd have to make damn sure he came in lowest. To do that, he needed to track down those other estimates. Starting with Robinson. He picked up the cell phone from the seat beside him, scrolled through the speed-dial list, and pressed a button.

"Hey, Dave, it's Chase," he said when the other man answered.

"Chase. What's up?"

"I need a huge favor."

"Sure. Shoot."

"I need to know what you bid on the Garrett job."

****

The next day Erika answered the phone on the first ring. "Hello?"

"Erika. It's Chase." As if the sexy tenor of his voice could belong to anyone else. "I have that proposal ready for you. I'm in the neighborhood, so would it be okay if I came over to drop it off?"

Interesting how he just happened to be so near. Coincidence? She didn't think so. At least he'd asked this time before showing up on her doorstep. "Sure." Might as well humor him.

He laughed. "You don't sound very enthusiastic." He paused. "Is this a bad time?"

"No, it's not that." Having him work for her topped the list of all time bad ideas. How could she explain it again? He hadn't paid any attention the first time. Or the second.

"You promised you'd take a look at my estimate,"

he said.

Damn. He'd always been able to read her mind.

"I can almost guarantee I'll be the lowest bid. And you said if I was, you'd hire me."

"I said I'd think about hiring you," she corrected.

She sensed his smile through the phone. "Same thing. I'll be there in five minutes."

Prompt as always, his truck pulled up in front of her house four-and-a-half minutes later. For the second time in the space of twenty-four hours, he stood on her doorstep.

"Hi," he said. "Long time no see."

She rolled her eyes. "Come on in."

He handed her an envelope. "Go ahead. Take a look." He looked smug.

She slid a fingernail beneath the sealed flap and pulled out the single sheet of paper. "Dammit," she muttered under her breath as she stared at the numbers on the page. True to his word, he had come in with the lowest bid. She nibbled on her nail.

"So?" The question sounded a little too innocent. He knew damn well his bid had come in the lowest. By far. "Do I get the job?"

Indecision knotted her stomach. With her finances in the shape they were, not accepting his bid would be financial suicide. From an economic standpoint, she *had* to hire Chase. She would be stupid not to. If he were anyone else, she wouldn't hesitate.

But it was Chase. What about their history? If she hired him she'd have to keep their relationship a business one. Client and contractor. Nothing more. Ignore her memories. Ignore the fact they used to be in-laws.

16

Ignore what her family would say. It shouldn't matter what they thought. Maybe they didn't even need to know. What if she kept the name of her carpenter a secret? She had her own life now, didn't she?

Still, the fear of Louise and Lauren finding out heightened her indecision. She didn't have time to psychoanalyze the deep roots of her fear while Chase stood in her hallway and waited for an answer. She couldn't make a decision yet.

She took a deep breath. "Can I think about it?"

He crossed his arms over his chest. "For how long?"

"Why are you being so pushy about this? Why do you want this job so badly?" Did he need the money?

"It isn't about the job, Erika." His intense gaze searched hers. "It's about you. Like I told you yesterday, I want to help you. Come on." His voice held a note of gentle persuasion. "Let me do this for you. For old times sake."

"Old times sake," she repeated in a whisper. She wavered.

As if sensing her weakening resolve, Chase added, "If I promise not to pressure you any more, do you promise to seriously consider letting me do the work for you?"

She closed her eyes. "Okay."

"Okay, you'll hire me?"

"Okay, I'll seriously consider it." She opened her eyes. "But give me a couple of days."

"I can do that." He held out his hand and said, formally, "Thank you for giving me the opportunity to be considered for your project."

She laughed despite the coil of tension in her

stomach and placed her hand in his. He clasped hers in a warm, firm grip, his palm rough against the smooth skin of her own. Heat raced up her arm and spread.

The tingling warmth suffused her body and forced her to admit her greatest fear. If she were honest with herself, her family finding out she wanted to hire Chase scared her a little, but didn't come close to what really frightened her.

The real problem was she'd never been able to forget how it felt to fall asleep in his arms.

Chapter Two

"Come on. It can't be that bad. It's summer vacation."

Erika raised her head from the cradle of her arms on the desk to offer a weary smile to Teri, her co-worker and friend.

"Don't be so sure."

Teri plopped down on an empty student desk. Her short, dark spiky hairdo and tiny form gave her the appearance of a pixie. "Talk to me."

"Honestly, I don't know where to start." Erika's gaze slid past Teri to the empty walls of the classroom. How bare they looked without the colorful bulletin boards and second grade artwork that had decorated them throughout the school year.

"How about at the beginning?"

Erika sighed, returning her attention to the other woman. "You know I have to have a bunch of work done at my new place?"

Teri nodded.

"Well, Chase somehow found out and came over to give me an estimate."

"Chase?"

"Lauren's ex? My brother-in-law." The label didn't fit any more, but what else could she call him?

Teri looked puzzled. "Okay." The word came out hesitantly, sounding like a question.

"See, he came in with the lowest bid. Of course he did," she muttered more to herself. "And I kind of said if he did I would consider hiring him."

Teri shook her head. "I'm not following you. That doesn't sound so bad. If he came in with the lowest bid, hire him."

Erika grimaced. "It's not as simple as it sounds. Lauren and Mom would have a fit if I hired him." No lie there, but something else made it more complicated than messed up family dynamics. Something Erika would never even tell her closest friend. Something that caused a blush to heat her cheeks and her heart to race. Something that still cost her sleep at night although nearly a year had passed.

"Things are that bad?"

"Worse than you can imagine. The only time Chase and Lauren even speak is when it has something to do with the girls. You should hear the things she says about him."

"Well, that's not good, but their relationship, or lack thereof, shouldn't have anything to do with you."

"I know. It's...it's a little more complicated than that." Seeing Chase every day would be sure to bring all of the old memories to the surface. They never hovered far beneath anyway. What would he say if he ever found out how often Erika thought about that night?

A concerned frown marred Teri's features, but to her credit, she didn't push Erika to reveal more. "Well, how much lower is his bid than the others? You could go with the next one in line."

"I know. That's what I should do." It would be the sane thing to do. She chewed a fingernail. "But, Teri, his estimate was *really* low. We're talking like a thousand dollars lower than the next guy."

Teri whistled. "Whew. That's not something you can easily dismiss."

"Tell me about it." She sighed. "Lauren and Louise have been through so much in the last few years. I don't want to hurt them more by going behind their backs and hiring Chase."

"Then don't go behind their backs. Tell them."

Erika shook her head. "I know it sounds stupid. And irrational. And crazy." Her smile was rueful. "But I honestly don't think that's a good idea." She grimaced. "Seriously, they hate him."

Teri rose and rested her hand on Erika's shoulder. "I wish I had better advice to give you. I know how close you are to Kevin's family, but a thousand dollars, that's huge."

"I know. I don't know what to do."

Teri squeezed her shoulder. "You'll figure something out. You always do."

"Yeah, I guess I'll have to."

Later that afternoon, despite the heat, Erika sat on the patio, the estimates from several contractors spread on the table, shaded by a large green market umbrella, in front of her. She avoided looking at the one sporting Chase's bold signature at the bottom. She willed the numbers on one of the others to change. To magically go below his.

She grimaced. Might as well wish on the pot of gold at the end of a rainbow. With a frustrated sigh, she pushed the papers away. Teri was right. Either she needed to simply accept Chase's bid and tell Louise and Lauren, or go with one of the others. And she had to make up her mind soon. The deadline enforced by the village wasn't getting any farther away.

Putting the decision off for a little while longer, she turned her attention to the day's mail she'd carried outside with her. She sorted the advertisements into one pile. Those would go right into the recycling bin. The stack grew as she added the junk mail. Which left only the bills.

Mostly the usual. Utilities. Car. Credit cards. She frowned at one with an unfamiliar return address and tucked a sweat-dampened strand of hair back into her ponytail. It looked too official to be junk mail. She slid a fingernail under the flap and tore the envelope open.

Her eyes widened at the amount due. She blinked and looked again. This couldn't be a bill for her. What had she spent twelve hundred dollars on? She double-checked the name and address. Definitely her.

Scanning the explanation of the charge, she groaned. Crap. The bill belonged to her all right. When she'd first moved in, she needed to replace the existing garage door and get a new opener. At the time, using one of those delayed payment plans with the home improvement store had seemed like a good idea. Now, too late, she questioned the wisdom of her decision. Where would she come up with an extra twelve hundred dollars?

Her gaze slid to the estimates she'd shoved to the side. Dammit. She rubbed her temples with her fingertips. Looked like a decision had been made for her.

****

At family dinner the next night, although the food smelled delicious, it all had the consistency of cardboard to Erika. The exuberant voices of the twins and the adults' conversation flowed around her, but she didn't take part. How in the world would she tell Louise and Lauren she'd decided to hire Chase to do the work on her house?

Might as well get it over with. She swallowed a tasteless bite of something—mashed potatoes?—then took a deep breath.

Before she could get the words out, Sami spoke up. "Mommy, I'm all done. Can I go play?"

"Me, too?" Steph chimed in.

"Did you finish your chicken?"

Chicken? Erika glanced down at her plate. One mystery solved.

"Yep. It's all gone. Can I go watch TV, pleeeeze?" Sami pleaded.

"Mine's gone, too," Steph added.

Lauren sighed, which ruffled the bangs of her straight, blonde hair. "Yes, you can go."

"Will you put *Little Mermaid* on?"

Lauren sighed again and tossed down her napkin. She pushed back her chair. "Sure." She followed the girls from the room.

Louise turned to Erika. "So, honey, you've been quiet tonight. What's going on?"

Louise had given her the perfect opening. She took a deep breath. Now or never. "Well, since school's out for the summer I can finally get to some of the work I need done around my new place. A lot of the inside stuff I can do myself, but I've been getting some estimates together for some of the bigger, outside projects."

"How's it coming?" Frank asked.

Erika swallowed. "Actually, I think I've decided on a contractor. He came in with the lowest bid—by far—and can get the job done in my timeframe."

"Did you ask for references?"

Her glance slid to the built-in bookcases in the living room. Chase had built them years ago. He'd also installed new cabinets in the kitchen. "I've seen some of his work. He's good."

Frank nodded. "You can't be too careful these days."

"Yeah, well that's why I decided to hire Ch—"

"If those two watch that movie one more time, they're going to turn into mermaids." Lauren plopped back down in her chair. "They even want to have a Little Mermaid birthday party. Which, by the way, I think Chase is going to be difficult about."

Erika snapped her mouth closed. Had her thoughts of Chase conjured his name from Lauren's lips? Her comment was completely out of the blue. Or had Erika missed something from an earlier conversation? She hadn't really been paying attention.

"Why would the kind of party they want matter to him?" Louise asked.

Lauren shook her head. "No, that's not what I meant. I want to have their party on the weekend before their birthday, and you know how he is about the custody arrangements. Not very flexible when it comes to his time with them. I'm sure he'll freak out when I tell him we're throwing the party on a weekend. Heaven forbid he ever give up one of his days with the girls."

Across the table, Frank looked up. "Why don't you invite him to the party?"

Lauren looked so aghast it was almost comical. "Ugh. Why would I do that?"

Frank sighed. "He's their father, Lauren. He has a right to be there. No matter what goes on between the two of you, you have to remember you have children together. And a responsibility to them. If only for their sakes, you and Chase have to be able to at least make an effort to get along."

"Don't you think I know that? We've been trying to figure out how to get along for a while now. Besides, why do you always defend him, Dad?"

He shook his head. "I'm not defending anyone. All I'm saying is inviting Chase to the party seems to be the best way to solve whatever the issue is."

Lauren wrinkled her nose. "This issue is I want to have a party for my daughters for their birthday."

"Of course you do, honey," Louise added her two cents to the conversation.

"And I'd rather he didn't come." Lauren looked down. "I want to invite Jim."

Erika hid her surprise. Lauren had been dating someone, but if she wanted to bring him to the birthday party, things must be getting more serious. Joining in family occasions was a big step.

Her reluctance to invite Chase made sense. Of course Lauren never needed an excuse to be upset or irritated with her ex-husband and vice versa. But inviting another man to his children's birthday party would be a sure way to set Chase off and start an argument.

Louise had brightened at the mention of Jim. "Well, that would be nice. It would be nice to get to know him better, especially if he's going to be a part of your life."

"Yeah, I think he is. I really like him." Lauren sighed and shook her head. "But I know Chase is going to be difficult about the whole thing."

"Chase will just have to get used to him being a part of your life. And the girls'. After all, he made the choice to not be a part of yours anymore."

"I know, but he's so damn stubborn." She put her elbows on the table and leaned in. "Enough about him. It makes me crazy just thinking about him. Erika, what's going on with you these days?"

"Oh, uh, nothing much," she stammered. No way in the world could she tell them about hiring Chase now. Maybe she wouldn't hire him after all. She'd crunch some numbers at home later and see if she could make another option work.

****

Erika resisted the urge to throw something. Barely. Crunching the numbers hadn't helped. Neither had cajoling, nudging, rearranging, or flat-out ordering them to come out differently. She had to face facts. From an economic standpoint, she had no choice but to hire Chase.

Maybe to some people, a thousand dollars one way or another wasn't a big deal. But in the last year she'd paid for hospital bills, funeral expenses, and the fees associated with selling and buying a house. Her savings account still hadn't recovered, and wouldn't for a long time.

Definitely not in time to meet the village's deadline. If she missed the date, it would mean more fees and fines. If Kevin had had life insurance, maybe things would be different. But he hadn't, and it would be fruitless to go down the shoulda/woulda/coulda path.

She yanked Chase's estimate toward her and glowered at it. Her head throbbed.

She needed to get it over with. Make the call. Do it and be done. Be strong and ignore the guilt of keeping something from her family. But no way would she tell them about hiring Chase. Unfortunately, it wasn't the first secret she'd ever kept from them.

Before she could wimp out, Erika dialed the number at the top of the page. She tapped the pen on the table while she waited for him to answer.

"Chase Stewart."

She ignored the tiny tingle just the sound of his voice elicited. "Hi, Chase, it's Erika."

"Hey there. How are you?"

"I'm fine." Not in the mood for pleasantries when her stomach was doing somersaults. "Look, I wanted to talk to you about your estimate."

"Sure. I can come by."

"Oh, no, you don't need to do that. We can talk about it on the phone."

"It's easier in person."

"Well, okay, if you want to come by tomorrow I should be here all day." If she put it off another day would she change her mind?

"Why don't I swing by tonight?"

She nibbled a fingernail. "I don't want to interrupt your evening at home."

"Actually, I haven't made it home yet. I worked late and stopped for a bite to eat, so it's no trouble. As long as I'm not interrupting your evening?"

"No, you wouldn't be." Other than catching up on the long list of shows on her DVR, she had no plans.

"Great. Then I'll see you in like half an hour?"

"Sure."

Thirty minutes later, her doorbell pealed. Right on time as always. She invited him in, ignoring the voice in the back of her head telling her how nice it would be to make a habit of opening the door to his smiling face.

She also ignored the hitch in her stomach his smile caused. Maybe dealing with the guilt of keeping secrets from her family would be easy compared to dealing with the guilt of inappropriate memories of him.

After she ushered him into the living room, he didn't waste any time, but got right down to business. "You said you had some questions about my estimate?"

"Not really a question." She paused and took a deep breath. "I've decided to hire you."

He grinned. "Fabulous. I'll—"

"I have one condition."

His eyes narrowed as his smile faded. He crossed his arms over his chest and leaned back against the couch cushions. "A condition?"

"Yes."

"All right. Let's hear it."

She stood to pace the length of the room and back. "If I hire you, you have to promise not to tell Mom or Lauren you're working here." She nibbled a thumbnail as she gauged his reaction.

"Why?"

She shook her head. "It's hard to explain."

"Try."

She stiffened at his tone. "Don't be difficult about this." It didn't escape her notice she'd used Lauren's words from earlier. "This was a really hard decision for me to make. But it's what I decided. So either you accept the job with my condition, or I find someone else." She held her breath. Would he call her bluff? With the garage door bill due, she couldn't afford anyone else's bid.

"Fine. I accept." He rose and held out his hand.

She hesitated a moment before placing hers in his warm, firm grasp. "Great. Then we have a deal."

"Yeah, I guess we do. But in my opinion, I think you should tell them."

She pulled her hand away and glared. "Will you be offering your opinion the whole time you're here?"

His lips quirked. "That depends."

She wanted to stamp her foot, but refrained from making the childish gesture. "On what?"

"Can I offer my opinion on paint choices and the type of wood to use?"

"I suppose." She bit back a smile. "Just remember to keep your opinions job-related. This is a business deal." She needed the reminder for herself as much as him.

He made a cross motion over his heart. "I promise. Do you want me to stick a needle in my eye, too?"

She laughed. "No, that won't be necessary. But if you're done giving me the third degree, let's get down to particulars. Is there something you want me to sign?"

He shook his head. "Do you really think I'm going to make you sign something?"

"Business, remember? You need to treat me like any other client."

"Fine. You can sign the proposal I gave you."

"Excellent. Do you want any money up front?"

"I usually ask for twenty-five percent of the total cost before I start a job, for materials and such. Does that work for you?"

She did a quick mental calculation. She'd have to play with the deadlines of some other bills. "I can make it work. What about permits?"

"We don't need a permit for the paint, but we do for the windows and the porch. I'll take care of it. I know the building commissioner in the village pretty well. I'll draw up the plans and submit them. I should be able to get the paperwork expedited pretty quickly. Maybe one or two days."

"Awesome. Anything else?"

"Nope, we're all set for now. I'll call you when I have the permits so we can set up a schedule. I'll probably be working your job and another one, if that's okay. There's something I have going right now I need to finish, so I won't be at your place everyday."

She frowned. "Are you sure you can get this done in my time frame? I mean," she clarified, "I'm not worried about my end so much as you putting other work aside for me."

"I'm not. I usually juggle a couple jobs at the same time. Oh, and I'll make some calls about the painting, so we can get that part of the project underway."

"Thank you."

"No problem."

On impulse, she touched his arm. The muscles were hard and firm beneath a light dusting of hair. "No, really. You have no idea how much I appreciate you being able to do this for me. At this price." She paused. "And with my condition."

His eyes crinkled when he smiled. "Like I said before. I'd do anything to help you."

****

Later at home, Chase mulled over his words. He hadn't lied. He would do anything to help Erika. But, if he were honest, the condition he'd agreed to bothered him. To be even more truthful, he couldn't say he had a problem lying to Lauren's family. It really wouldn't be lying. As long as he paid Lauren her monthly child support payments, she shouldn't care less who he worked for. Outside of matters concerning Steph and Sami, he and Lauren's parents weren't really on a chit-chatty enough basis for the subject of his job to even come up.

What bothered him, although he couldn't put his finger on exactly why, was how keeping secrets from Lauren's family would affect Erika. Why would she want to lie to them? Was it so awful to have hired him? And if she was so determined to keep it a secret, why had she hired him in the first place? She'd had other options.

True, he'd low-balled his bid, but she still could have gone with another contractor. Made her life a little bit easier. She'd told him how hard the decision had been to make. And he'd seen it in her eyes as well. Lauren or Louise finding out made her nervous.

So despite the uneasy feeling in the pit of his stomach, he'd do his part to make sure they didn't. He didn't want to make Erika's life any more difficult.

Chapter Three

"Erika?" Chase's voice called from inside the house. The screen door squealed in its track.

"Out here." She looked up from her glass of wine when he walked out onto the small patio.

He winced. "That needs some oil." His boots made a hollow sound against the pavers as he made his way toward her. "I'm guessing that door isn't original to the house?"

She laughed. "Probably a good guess. One of these days I'll replace it. Maybe with French doors?"

He nodded. "That would be nice. At any rate, I wanted to let you know I'm done for the day."

"Oh, okay." She swirled the red liquid in the glass and contemplated its motion.

"Is something wrong?"

"What? Oh, no. Just thinking about some things." Him actually. She'd dreamed about him last night. A dream she hadn't been quite able to hang onto once she'd awakened, although it had left her feeling strangely restless.

"Want to talk about it?"

She looked up at him and smiled. "No, thanks." She swept her hand out, indicating the chair across from her. "Want to join me for a glass of wine? Or would you rather have a beer?"

"No, a glass of wine sounds nice." The metal legs

scraped across the bricks as he pulled the chair out.

She smiled again. "I love that sound. It's a summer sound."

He reached for the empty glass and filled it, then raised it toward her in a toast. "Thanks. This is nice." He stretched his feet out in front of him and crossed them at the ankles. With a contented sigh, he tilted his head back to gaze up at the darkening sky.

"It's getting late. You work too hard." He'd been working at her house on and off for the last couple of weeks. Unless he had the girls, most nights he stayed until dusk.

His gaze met hers. "I want to be sure to get everything done by the deadline."

"You're a good guy, Chase."

"I try." His expression turned wry. "Contrary to popular family belief."

Erika gazed at him through the flame of the Citronella candle on the table between them. The flare flickered, set in motion by the warm breeze as it rustled through the nearby trees. It reflected in the deep pools of his eyes, making them look dark and mysterious in the dim twilight.

Fragments of her dream came back. She cleared her throat and looked away. "Are you hungry? I can make you something."

"I'm good. I took a break around six and had a sandwich."

"That can't be very filling."

"You don't know how I make my sandwiches." He grinned.

"Still. That's not a very good supper. Tell you what, tomorrow I'll make you dinner."

He shook his head. "I don't want you to go to any trouble."

"It's no trouble. Really, it's just as easy, maybe easier, to cook for two instead of one." The attempt to convince him triggered a little voice in her head. Making him dinner would belie the carefully constructed lines of their relationship she'd drawn, if only in her own mind. Cooking for him went beyond the bounds of normal customer-contractor interaction. Of course, dreaming about him did, too.

"You don't need to make me dinner."

"I want to." The lines were getting fuzzier.

"Okay, but if you're providing dinner, then I'm knocking some money from my quote."

"No, you're not." Her voice was adamant. "You can't be making very much on this job as it is. Your bid was ridiculously below anyone else's." She shook her head, even though the relatively low cost of his work was saving her butt. She hoped it wasn't too much of a hardship. He had to have bills to pay like she did. And child support on top of everything else.

"I had to make sure you'd give me the job." He winked. "And besides, I told you there would be a family discount."

She crossed her arms over her chest. "Fine. If this is going to be a family thing, then me cooking dinner for you isn't a problem." Nothing like throwing her boundaries completely out the window.

He grinned and raised his glass. "Touché." His eyes focused on the sky again. Stars were beginning to dot the dark expanse. "Do you remember that one Thanksgiving when everyone else fell asleep after dinner, and you and I went outside to talk?"

She laughed. "How could I forget? It was freezing, but we didn't want to wake everyone up."

"The stars were out that night, too."

"I don't remember the stars. I only remember how cold it was. What were we thinking?"

He smiled. "I don't know, but it was nice talking to you." His gaze found hers. "It's always nice talking to you. I miss that."

"Me, too." She looked away from the intensity in his eyes.

The night settled more completely, blanketing them in its velvety darkness. Lightning bugs glowed on and off out in the yard.

"So I—" The phone rang, interrupting whatever he'd been going to say.

"Sorry, just a sec." She clicked the Talk button. "Hello?"

"Hi, honey, it's Mom."

Erika's gaze darted to Chase. "Hi, Mom."

"What are you up to tonight?"

She looked away from the man across from her. "Just sitting outside, enjoying the evening."

"It is lovely out. What did you do today?"

"Nothing too exciting. I'm enjoying my time off."

Louise chuckled. "Yes, you're always good for the first couple weeks of summer vacation. And then boredom sets in."

Erika laughed and hoped the other woman wouldn't hear the self-conscious edge to it. "Oh, you know me well."

"You bet I do, but I won't keep you from your evening. I have the day off on Thursday, so Lauren is bringing the girls over for lunch. I wondered if you'd like to join us."

"I'd love to. Can I bring anything?"

"Of course not, just yourself, honey."

"Okay, I'll see you then."

"Bye, hon."

Erika clicked the phone off then set it back on the table. She sipped her wine. The glass trembled in her hand. After what seemed like a lifetime, she found the courage to glance up at Chase.

He wasn't looking at her. With the tip of his index finger, he traced the diamond pattern of the metal table.

"That, um, that was Mom."

His mouth quirked. "So I gathered."

"Thanks for not saying anything to let her know someone else was here."

His severe gaze met hers. "Do you really think I would do that?"

"No." Of course she knew better. Despite what Lauren may claim to the contrary, Chase wouldn't do something spiteful on purpose. She blew out a breath. "I know. I'm sorry."

He waved off the apology. "So you haven't told them anything about the work going on around here?"

"They know I'm having the work done. That's about it."

"It's hard for you, keeping a secret from them." It wasn't a question.

"Yes."

"You've done it before, though, haven't you?" The words were soft, but his astute gaze met hers.

A tremor went through her. The breath caught in her throat. He couldn't mean what she thought he did. Could he? How could he possibly know? But staring into his all too perceptive eyes, suddenly she had no doubt he did.

She looked away. Swallowed. "O...of course not."

"Erika." His voice was low. Compelling. Sympathetic.

"I..." she faltered.

"You never told them about Kevin, did you?"

Her gaze returned to his. She shook her head in a helpless gesture. How could she answer? How could he know to ask?

"About where he was coming from the night he was killed. He was coming from another woman's house, wasn't he?"

The words took her breath away, like a punch to her midsection. For a moment she couldn't move. Couldn't speak. Couldn't breathe. Finally she sucked in several shuddering breaths and found her voice. "H-how did you know?"

Chase shrugged. "Just a hunch." He paused. "So, I'm right?"

"I don't know," she whispered. "I only had a hunch, too."

"For how long?"

Now she shrugged. "A year or so before he died. Maybe longer," she said softly.

"More than a year?" His voice held equal parts frustration and empathy. "Why didn't you ever confront him?"

"I didn't know for sure. What if I was wrong? I mean, at first, I was naive enough to believe the lies he told me about working late and the business trips. For a while I even admired his dedication to his job. Of course when I finally wised up and figured out what was really going on, all those behaviors and excuses taunted me and reminded me how stupid I'd been."

Silence fell. Cicadas buzzed in the stillness.

After a long while, he reached across the table and placed his hand over hers. Warmth, different than the summer heat, stole through her. Beneath the flare of awareness, the ache in her heart eased. Why did his touch always bring such comfort?

"You never told anyone, did you? You carried it all inside."

"I was too embarrassed and humiliated. How could I admit I'd been naive for so long? I believed all his lies. And I was scared."

"Scared?"

"Of losing my family."

Chase looked thoughtful, but didn't comment. "When did you really figure it out?"

"Not too long before the accident. He got careless. I guess by then he didn't care if he got caught. I tried to work up the courage to confront him, but before I could, he died."

Chase shook his head. "The bastard is lucky he's dead, or I might want to kill him myself." The harsh words were a direct contrast to the soft brush of his fingers on the back of her hand.

"You shouldn't say things like that."

"Even now, after he's been gone almost a year, you're still living the lie. Defending him. Covering for him."

"What else can I do?"

"You don't think Louise and Frank should know?"

"No." The word was vehement. "They wouldn't believe it anyway. He was the golden child. Perfect in their eyes." She looked up at Chase. "And now that he's gone, what purpose would it serve to taint their memory of him? They've been through so much these last couple of years. Your and Lauren's separation and divorce, Kevin's death. Why add to the hurt?"

"He hurt you."

"So that makes it okay to turn around and hurt someone else? They don't deserve that."

His fingers stroked over her knuckles. She shivered. "That's the real reason why you don't want them to know I'm working here, isn't it? You're afraid of hurting them."

She looked at him and managed half a smile. "Boy, you're perceptive tonight." Her gaze shifted to their hands, twined together on the table. "They've been so good to me. Especially Louise. She treats me like I'm her daughter. Her real daughter. No one ever did before." Her voice broke. His hand tightened.

"My own mother left me when I was barely two. I don't even remember her. As for the rest of my dad's wives, they treated me as more of an inconvenience than a stepdaughter. They only put up with me because I was a package deal with my dad. They never loved me.

"But Kevin's mom did. The first time he brought me home to meet his family, they welcomed me with open arms. Accepted me. Loved me. They still do. Even though he's gone, I'm still part of their family. Still their daughter. They're my only real family. I can't lose them."

Her words lingered in the dark of the night.

When the silence became too much, she pulled her hand from his to wipe away her tears. She hadn't meant to cry. "God." The harsh word echoed in the darkness. "I'm so sorry. I don't know what's the matter with me. You didn't need to hear all that."

"Erika." His voice held a soft reprimand. "Don't ever apologize for telling me how you feel. You know you can tell me anything. I'll always listen. Or be there when you need a shoulder to cry on."

She couldn't meet his eyes. She vividly recalled another time he'd offered a shoulder to cry on. And she accepted. Countless people had come to Kevin's wake and funeral, offering condolences, asking what they could do to help. They'd all seemed like empty words. The only real comfort she found had been in Chase's arms.

The memory brought more snatches of last night's elusive dream. Their emotional conversation had driven it from her mind for a while, but now once again it teased her with its reluctance to be fully remembered.

She shook her head to chase away the disturbing, half-formed images.

"Are you going to be okay?" The soft words curled around her.

"Yeah, I am."

"I'm sorry I brought it up. I didn't mean to make you sad."

"I know." For the first time in long minutes she looked up and met his eyes. "To be honest, it's kind of a relief having someone else know." An unexpected wave of weariness washed over her. She couldn't suppress a yawn.

Chase's chair scraped the bricks as he stood. "It's late. I should get going."

She rose as well. "I'll walk you out."

He shook his head. Smiled. "I can find my own way." He reached out to tuck a strand of hair behind her ear. She shivered at the gentle touch against her skin. Her mouth went dry as she gazed up into his enigmatic eyes. She wished she could read his mind.

His head lowered. A portion of her dream came back in sudden, vibrant detail. His warm, wine-scented breath fanned her face as he pressed a kiss to her forehead. "See you tomorrow."

She dropped lifelessly back into her chair after he'd gone. For a moment there, a wonderful, pulse-pounding, heart-stopping moment, she thought he was going to kiss her. Really kiss her.

Like he had in her dream.

Her thoughts skidded to a stop, and she backpedaled through the last five seconds in her mind. *Wonderful?*

Had she wanted Chase to kiss her? She pressed trembling fingers to her lips to stifle a small moan. She had. Had wanted it badly.

With a groan, she buried her face in her hands. She shouldn't want Chase to kiss her. Shouldn't yearn for him to do so. Shouldn't long to feel his arms around her again.

Had he known? Tomorrow, when he returned, would he be able to tell? Would she be able to hide her inappropriate desire, or would it be visible on her face?

She needed to find an excuse to be out of the house. Certainly she had errands to run to keep her busy for most of the day. Or perhaps Teri would be up for some shopping.

She glanced at the outdoor clock on the back wall. As a certified night owl, Teri wouldn't mind a phone call this late.

The other woman answered on the third ring. Her voice sounded groggy.

"Hey, Teri, it's Erika. Did I wake you?"

"Not really. I was watching TV and kind of drifted off a little."

"Oh, sorry."

"No problem. I'd have a stiff neck if I laid there any longer. So what's up?"

"I know this is last minute, but I wondered if you were up for a girls' day out tomorrow. I thought maybe brunch and then we could get our nails done and do some shopping?"

"Sounds perfect. Do you want me to come get you in the morning?"

"No, I'll swing by and pick you up. I'm going to get up early and run some errands first." She wanted to be long gone by the time Chase arrived.

****

The next morning Erika left a note and a key in an envelope taped to the door. Her day out kept her away from the house, but even indulging in girl talk and shoe shopping hadn't been enough to take her mind off of Chase completely. Memories of their conversation, her dream, and his almost kiss drifted through her thoughts in an endless loop. If Teri noticed her perpetual distraction, God bless her, she didn't comment.

On the way home, she stopped for groceries. On and off throughout the day she'd considered calling Chase and telling him she couldn't make dinner for him after all, but something had always stopped her before she reached for the phone.

She turned into the driveway and steered around

his truck to pull into the garage. Her heart spattered a disjointed rhythm, and she hesitated before getting out. She sucked a breath into her lungs. Too late to back out now. With firm resolve, she pushed open the door, and then headed inside.

She nodded at Chase, who was working on the bay windows on the back of the house. Ignoring the skittish way her pulse sped, she unpacked the ingredients for a simple meal of salad, pasta, and garlic bread.

A tuneless song hummed through her lips as she put the water on to boil. It had been a long time since she'd fixed dinner for a man. Or anyone. The prospect of having someone to eat with put a spring in her step. Other than family dinners over at Louise and Frank's, most nights she ate alone.

She set napkins and plates on the blue-checked cloth that covered table along with the silverware, then added a wine glass at each place. She nibbled on her fingernail, then remembered the new polish and shoved her hands in the back pockets of her shorts. Should she add candles?

No, of course not. Too romantic. She and Chase were simply two people who happened to be at the same place sharing a meal. Friends—acquaintances— wouldn't have a candlelit dinner.

She tore the lettuce into small pieces, and then tossed it into a bowl before adding sliced tomatoes and cucumbers. When the timer dinged, she slid the garlic bread into the oven. The spaghetti needed only a few more minutes, and the sauce bubbled on the stove when the squeal of the screen door announced Chase's presence.

A knot of nerves settled in her stomach. Her smile

only trembled slightly when she turned to greet him. "Hi. Dinner's about ready."

He came closer and sniffed appreciatively. "Smells delicious. I hope you didn't go to too much trouble." He leaned against the counter next to the stove. The pose thrust his hips forward.

She looked away and busied herself with the spaghetti. "Not at all. I told you, cooking for both of us is just as easy as cooking for me. I hope pasta is okay?" She risked a glance at him.

"Perfect." He paused. "You weren't around much today."

She turned back to the stove to evade his perceptive eyes. Had he guessed she'd been avoiding him? Hadn't wanted to be around for fear he'd be able to read the yearning in her eyes. The desire to feel his lips against hers. To taste him. She swallowed. "Yeah, um, a girlfriend and I spent the afternoon doing girly things, and in the morning I had a lot of errands to run." Her excuses sounded lame, so before he could question her further, she changed the subject. "How are those windows coming?"

"Great. I'm almost done with the back. I figured I'd take a little break for dinner, and then finish up the last one before I head home for the day."

She shook her head. "You work too hard."

He shrugged and glanced at the stove. "I should wash up a bit before we eat."

She nodded. Her gaze lingered on the sway of his hips as he strolled from the room. The buzz of the timer made her jump.

She pulled the bread from the oven, sliced it, and set it on the table in a basket. Bowls of steaming pasta and sauce followed. Last, she removed the salad from the fridge, and then added the dressing.

She surveyed the table. What was missing? She snapped her fingers. The wine.

She recorked the bottle as Chase walked back into the kitchen. He held his cell phone pressed to his ear. "No, of course I'll come get them. I'll be there as soon as I can." He snapped the phone closed. He surveyed the table, then turned to Erika. Regret filled his eyes.

No. The silent denial echoed in her head.

He pinched the bridge of his nose between thumb and forefinger. "Erika, I'm so sorry." He waved his hand over the table. "This all looks wonderful, but I can't stay."

Memories she'd rather forget peppered her mind. Kevin calling to cancel dinner plans. Calling to say he'd be late. Calling to lie about his whereabouts.

The lump in her throat threatened to choke her. She swallowed and it settled in her stomach. "I...is something the matter?"

"No, nothing's wrong. That was Lauren. She's going out tonight, and her babysitter came down with the flu. I need to pick up the girls."

"Oh. Okay. Well, as long as nothing's wrong." She looked down at her toes, unable to meet his gaze. Would he hear the slight tremor in her voice?

"Erika."

She glanced up at him.

"I really am sorry."

She forced a smile. "I know." She straightened her shoulders. "Don't worry about it. You, uh, should get going. You don't want to keep the girls waiting."

"Okay." The screen door squealed in its track as he

opened it. She winced at the harsh sound, loud in the uncomfortable silence. He turned, hesitated before he spoke. "I'm not sure when I'll be here tomorrow. I'm keeping the girls overnight. Lauren will get them in the morning, but she didn't give me a specific time."

She waved a hand. "No problem. Whenever is fine." She hugged herself.

"I'll see you tomorrow, then."

Erika nodded.

The door grated shut. She flinched. Outside, his truck roared to life, then backed out of the driveway. The rumble of its engine faded as he drove away.

She released a shaky sigh. Her gaze slid over the table laden with food. No sense wasting it. She sat down and pulled the napkin onto her lap. After dishing up generous helpings of salad and pasta, she rolled some noodles onto her fork, then popped it into her mouth.

The food had no taste. In disgust she scraped the unappealing meal into the disposal. The growl of its motor echoed in the too silent kitchen. Her plate clattered into the sink. A tear slipped down her cheek.

She brushed it away with a quick, jerky swipe of her fingers. Chase needing to pick up the twins was not the same as Kevin canceling plans to spend time with someone else. But old hurts stung.

Not the same. Not the same. Not the same. The mantra reverberated in her head.

Chase had left to take care of his daughters, not to be with another woman. Besides, even if he had left for the company of someone else, why should it matter? She'd hired him as a contractor. Nothing more.

She dashed away the moisture on her cheek with

the back of her hand. Wasn't she beyond tears? She'd shed enough over Kevin, and there was no reason to cry over Chase.

No reason at all.

****

Chase's stomach growled, reminding him he hadn't eaten. Reminding him he'd hurt Erika.

She'd tried to hide it. To act like his skipping out on dinner hadn't bothered her. But he'd seen the look in her eyes. Pain he put there. He cursed under his breath.

"What, Daddy?"

"Nothing, Steph." He shook his head to clear the disturbing thoughts. "What jammies do you want to wear tonight?"

"Little Mermaid."

He chuckled. "Wow, what a surprise." He turned to his other daughter. "What about you, Sami?"

Her brow furrowed as she thought. "Me, too," she finally decided.

"Little Mermaid it is." He slipped the matching nightgowns over the girls' heads. "Now scoot to the bathroom and brush your teeth."

"I bet I can win," Steph cried.

"Nooooo, I can win." Sami pushed past her sister on the way out the door.

"Hey, no arguing. And no pushing. You can both win," Chase called.

From the bathroom, their voices drifted into the bedroom.

"Don't squeeze it so hard."

"I didn't."

"I get to turn it on." Water splashed into the sink.

"I'll turn it off."

"I'm not done yet."

The familiar banter curled into his heart, erasing some of the guilt of leaving Erika. An ache he didn't want to analyze.

"We're done," Steph announced as they skipped back into the room.

"Sami, why don't you pick a book while I brush Steph's hair?"

"Okay." Sami plopped in front of the bookcase.

"C'mere, Steph." Chase settled her onto his lap where he sat cross-legged on the floor. He pulled the brush through her long, dark hair with smooth, even strokes. The sweet scent of baby shampoo filled his nostrils. He plaited her hair into a braid, the soft strands slipping easily through his fingers then kissed the top of her head. "Next."

Sami scooted over to take her sister's place. When he finished with her hair, she turned and wrapped her arms around his neck. "I love you, Daddy."

He hugged her close. "I love you, too."

"Me too, me too." Steph scrambled onto his lap to join the family huddle.

Two warm bodies wiggled against him. Four small arms squeezed his neck. Minty breath whispered over his face. Chase closed his eyes. He doubted any other man on earth could be as happy as this. Contentment washed through him and filled his soul. Except for the tiny part where the thought of Erika lingered.

He squeezed the twins one more time and opened his eyes. "Okay, so what stories do we have for tonight?"

"*Huggsie the Penguin*," Sami said.

Steph held up her book. "*ABC's*."

"Ah, two of my favorites."

"You always say that." Steph rolled her eyes.

He laughed and scooted backwards until he rested against Sami's bed. The twins snuggled in on either side as he opened the first book.

Both girls were heavy-lidded with sleep by the time he closed the second. He kissed the tops of their heads in turn. "Okay, time for bed."

Groans met his announcement. "But I'm not tired," Steph protested. A yawn garbled the words.

He smiled. "Humor me." He tucked both girls into bed, listened to their prayers, and kissed each forehead. At the door he turned. "I love you."

"I love you, Daddy." The words slurred.

"I love you, too," Sami echoed.

"See you in the morning." He clicked off the light and then softly closed the door.

In the kitchen, he opened the fridge. A half-used jar of spaghetti sauce taunted him from the top shelf. He cursed and slammed the door shut. Should he call Erika? Would it make things worse?

She answered right away. "Hello?"

"It's Chase."

"Hi."

He cleared his throat. "I wanted to call and apologize again."

"You didn't need to do that." But she sounded pleased he had. She paused. "Did you have fun with the girls?"

"Always. I just tucked them into bed." He hesitated. "Would it be out of line to ask for a rain check on dinner for tomorrow night?"

Erika laughed. "No, of course not. But I can't

tomorrow."

She had plans? A date? With whom? He ignored the inappropriate stab of jealousy. "No rush." He hoped his voice sounded even.

"I don't mind making dinner for you, but I'm going to Mom's tomorrow for lunch, and I don't know how long I'll be."

His relief shouldn't have been so profound. What did it matter if she had a date? "Oh, right. You mentioned the other day you were having lunch with Lauren and the girls over there."

"You remembered?" Once again an underlying note of satisfaction laced her voice.

"Of course. Listen, I won't keep you. Like I said, I wanted to apologize again."

"Thank you."

"Will I see you tomorrow?"

"Probably not. I won't get home from Mom and Dad's until later."

He tamped down his disappointment. "All right, then I'll see you on Friday. Good night, Erika."

Chapter Four

Erika arrived at her mother-in-law's house right before Lauren and the girls. Lauren immediately shooed the twins to the playroom downstairs, then sank onto the couch. She leaned her head against the cushions, closed her eyes, and groaned.

Erika glanced over. "You don't look so good."

The other woman yawned. "I'm just tired." She opened her eyes. "And a little hung over. I think I overdid it on the sangria last night."

"Where did Jim take you?" Louise asked.

"This great little Mexican place."

"Did Tina have the girls?"

Lauren shook her head. "No, she came down with the flu, so Chase took them overnight."

"Well, that worked out nicely."

Erika grimaced. Sure it worked out nicely. For everyone except her.

"Yeah, I have to give Chase credit there. He never turns down the chance to spend time with the girls. I swear he has no other life." She sat up. "Although, when I called and asked him, at first he sounded strange."

"Strange? How so?" Louise asked.

"Well, I got the sense I'd interrupted something."

Louise raised an eyebrow.

Lauren waved a hand. "No, nothing like that. But I

did wonder if he had someone with him."

Erika examined a minute chip in the lime green nail polish on her pinky finger as a blush heated her cheeks.

"Well, honey, you're dating Jim. Does it bother you Chase might be dating someone, too?"

What would it be like to date Chase? Where would he take her? He liked Mexican food. Maybe they could try out the same place Lauren and Jim had gone.

Lauren snorted. "Bother me? No. But I guess it does surprise me. His whole life revolves around the girls. I don't know why any woman would be willing to take a backseat to that."

Erika ignored the tiny ache that grabbed her heart and put a stop to her brief flight of fancy. Nope. She wouldn't be dating Chase. For a plethora of reasons.

"I really don't care what he does," Lauren said. "I—"

"Mommy." The twins raced into the room. Steph held a book in her hand. "Will you read us a story?"

Lauren winced and rubbed her temples. "Shhhh. Not so loud."

"Will you read a story?" Sami's attempt at a whisper wasn't much softer than her sister's exuberance.

"Not right now, sweetie. Maybe later." Lauren stood. "I need a cup of coffee. Do you have any, Mom?"

"Of course." The two women left the room.

Erika turned to the twins, who sported identical pouts. "Come here, I'll read to you."

"You will?"

"You bet." She patted the sofa next to her. "Climb

up."

"Can we both sit by you? That's how we read with Daddy."

"Sure."

They snuggled in on either side.

"Sometimes we read two books," Steph hinted.

"Read this one first," Sami said. "It's about a lizard named Leonard."

"Yeah, that's a funny one."

The girls giggled as Erika read about Leonard and his antics. When she closed the book, Sami handed her another one. This time the adventures of Fall Guy, the Autumn Bear captured their attention.

"That guy is so silly," Steph said when they finished.

Erika hugged her. "He is pretty hilarious." If one appreciated four-year-old humor.

"We read two stories with Daddy last night, too. He always reads us two stories before we go to bed."

"Yeah, Mommy went out with Jim. Tina was s'posed to come over, but she got sick. So we got to have a sleepover at Daddy's." Excitement laced Steph's voice.

Sami shifted to her knees and bounced on the couch. "Yeah, and it wasn't even Saturday."

Erika's heart contracted at the girls' enthusiasm. How selfish of her to begrudge them time with their father. "Did you have fun with your daddy?"

"We always have fun with Daddy. Last night he made us grilled cheese for dinner and we got to play outside with him for a little and inside we played another a game and then—"

"Then," Sami cut in, "after we put our jammies on

he braided our hair and read us *two* stories." She wrinkled her nose. "But then we had to go to bed."

Erika's earlier irritation melted away, leaving guilt in the place of her selfishness. The girls obviously derived as much pleasure from being with Chase as he did from spending time with them.

"That does sound like fun."

Sami nodded. "Daddy's a good braider. See?" She turned her head to display her neatly plaited hair.

"Very nice." Erika imagined the satisfaction the simple task would bring Chase.

Steph climbed off the couch and grabbed Erika's hand. "Do you want to play a game?"

Erika allowed herself to be hauled to her feet. "I'd love to play a game."

"Can we play the one with the cherries?" Sami asked.

"Whatever you want." With a small hand tucked into each of her own, Erika headed toward the playroom, her thoughts on the man the girls so resembled.

After a while Lauren joined them. "Thanks." She nodded toward the game spread on the floor between Erika and the girls.

"It's no problem. I'm having fun." She spun the arrow on the spinner, then removed the proper number of cherries from her tree. "Your turn, Sami."

"You're so patient with them," Lauren said. "Sometimes I want to tear my hair out."

"I don't get to see them every day. You're with them all the time. It makes a difference," Erika said.

Lauren remained silent for a moment. "Chase is fabulous with them."

Erika looked up in surprise. Lauren hardly ever had anything nice to say about Chase.

Her expression must have given her away, because Lauren laughed. "I know I gripe about him a lot, but he's really a great father. When they're with him, he devotes all his attention to them." Lauren guided Steph through her turn before continuing. "Sometimes I think they'd be better off with Chase during the week and me on the weekends. But changing things around wouldn't really work for our schedules right now."

"Aunt Erika, your turn," Sami prodded.

Erika dutifully took her turn, but her mind wandered far from the colorful game in front of her. She couldn't imagine anything in the world Chase would want more than to spend extra time with his girls.

His daughters were his priority. His life. Lauren was right about one thing. What woman could compete with that kind of love?

Certainly not Erika. Been there, done that. Never again.

****

The next night, right around dinnertime, Erika's doorbell pealed. She frowned. Who could it be? Chase was out back working on one of the windows. What if it were Louise and Frank? Or Lauren?

No, her family didn't usually stop by unannounced. Thank goodness. Otherwise she'd never have been able to hire Chase, and, after seeing the work he'd done on the house so far, despite all of the indecision and sleepless nights it had caused, the decision had been the right one.

She set the brush across the can then climbed down

the ladder where she'd been painting a corner of the living room. Instead of dingy white, the walls were now the rich burnt orange of a sunset. She wiped her hands down her paint-splotched jeans, tucked a strand of hair behind her ear, and stood on tip toe to peek through one of the small windows at the top of the door. A pizza delivery boy stood on the porch.

He greeted her with a smile when she swung the door open. "That'll be fifteen-fifty."

She shook her head. "I'm sorry, you must have the wrong house. I didn't—"

"I've got it." Chase spoke from behind her.

She glanced over her shoulder as he pulled his wallet out of his back pocket.

"How much was it?"

"Fifteen-fifty," the boy repeated. He handed Chase the box.

Chase gave him a twenty-dollar bill. "Keep the change."

"Thanks. Enjoy your pizza." He turned and bounded down the stairs.

Erika closed the door and pivoted to face Chase. She raised an eyebrow.

He smiled and traced a finger down her cheek. It came away with a dab of paint clinging to the tip. He nodded toward the living room. "That's looking nice."

"Thanks. I'm not a professional, but it'll do. I just have one small area to finish." She nodded toward the box. "What's with the pizza?"

He slung an arm around her shoulders. Her heart jolted. "I still feel bad about ditching you the other night. Pizza is my lame way of trying to make it up to you."

She laughed, even though the simple gesture made her feel all mushy inside. "Sounds good to me."

"Tell you what, I'll put this in the oven to keep it warm. You finish that corner while I clean up for the day, and I'll meet you on the patio in say, fifteen minutes?"

She eyed the remaining portion of the wall needing paint. "Better make it twenty. At least." To say she wasn't the world's speediest painter was an understatement. But, she was enjoying the task and the accompanying sense of pride from making the house her own. She'd started with the master bedroom where the now soothing light turquoise blue walls and contrasting brown bedding provided a personal, cozy oasis.

After finishing and cleaning up, she glanced at the clock over the sink. Not too bad. Only ten minutes longer than she'd promised. She hoped Chase wasn't too hungry. She poured two glasses of lemonade, tucked plates and napkins under her arm, and nudged the screen door open with her elbow.

He glanced up as she walked out onto the patio. She handed him the glasses, before turning to close the door. When she looked back at him, he was watching her, an expectant look on his face.

"What?" She glanced at the table. He hadn't started on the pizza. "Oh, you didn't need to wait for me. I'm sure you're hungry."

"I didn't mind waiting." His lips quirked.

She wondered about the small smile as she pulled out a chair. Was she missing something?

"Do you by chance have any hot sauce?"

She stopped midway down. "I'm not sure. I'll

check." She slid the door open. As she stepped over the threshold, it dawned on her. It hadn't grated in the track. She spun to face Chase.

He grinned broadly. "Took you long enough."

"How did you fix it?"

"I oiled it. That thing was driving me crazy."

"Thank you."

"You're welcome. Now sit down and eat." He waved the pizza he held in his hand.

"Let me get your hot sauce first."

"Erika, I didn't really want hot sauce."

She glanced over at the door and smiled sheepishly. "Oh. Right."

"You don't have the girls tonight?" she asked after taking the edge off her hunger with a piece of extra cheesy gooey pizza.

"No, I only have them every other Friday."

"They were telling me how much fun they had with you on Wednesday."

He looked pleased. "Yeah, we do have a lot of fun." His eyes held hers. "But I wish I hadn't had to ditch out on dinner with you. I really am so—"

"Chase, you need to stop apologizing. The girls are your priority." She offered a smile to hide the jealous twinge in her heart. "That's how it should be."

He held her gaze for a moment longer before nodding.

They devoured most of the pizza in record time. As they both reached for the last piece, their hands collided.

"Ooops, sorry," Erika said. "I—"

Instead of pulling back, Chase twined his fingers with hers. He twisted their hands so hers faced up.

"Blue?"

"What?"

He wiggled their joined hands. "Your nails."

"Oh, yeah," she said with a self-conscious grin. "It's an indulgence."

"Are they always blue?"

She laughed, although her pulse had quickened at the touch of his skin against hers. "No, of course not. Sometimes they're purple, or green, or pink." Her nail biting habit necessitated changing the color often.

"I bet your kids at school love it."

"Yeah, I guess they do." She looked down at their intertwined fingers. "Kevin hated it when I got the bright colors." The words slipped out before she could stop them. She glanced up at Chase. A tiny frown marred his forehead. "He, uh, he always said it didn't look proper on someone my age."

Chase studied her for the space of several heartbeats. "I like them."

Silence fell. Grew. A warm breeze ruffled the remains of their meal. Heat tingled in her fingertips and spread, until her whole body hummed with an acute awareness of his touch.

Her dreams would be vivid tonight. Maybe putting the past to rest would help. The way his touch burned into her, she doubted it, but it was worth a shot. She took a deep breath. "Do you remember Kevin's funeral?"

If the question took him by surprise, he didn't show it. "Of course."

"Why did you come over afterwards?"

"You looked like you needed a shoulder to cry on." He smoothed his thumb over her knuckles. "All day.

During the wake. The funeral. You never shed one tear. You wore a brave face. Held it together. Were so strong." His gaze met hers. "And I didn't want you to be alone in an empty house."

Erika nodded. Her throat clogged with remembered tears. Not for Kevin, but for the sincerity and kindness of Chase's gesture. "I-I was surprised you came to the funeral at all. You and Lauren were already divorced by then."

"I didn't come for her. I came for you. I knew I couldn't change anything, or do anything, but I wanted to be there."

Her breath caught at the admission. "You did more than you'll ever know."

"Did you ever tell anyone—Lauren? Louise?—I came over that night?"

She raised an eyebrow. "Are you kidding? Mom and Lauren would have heart failure if they knew you spent the night with me after Kevin's funeral." She shuddered.

He chuckled. "You make it sound so sordid. It's not like anything happened." He squeezed her hand. "You cried and then fell asleep in my arms."

Nothing had happened, but her heart stuttered in an irregular rhythm at the memory of his arms around her. She'd never forgotten. Probably because she thought about it way too often. Especially these days with Chase there so much. "I know, but seriously, can you imagine what their reaction would have been if they'd seen you sneaking out of my house in the middle of the night? What they'd say if they found out now? Or if they saw us," she glanced at their joined hands, "like this."

"For the record. I didn't sneak."

Erika laughed, but looked away from his teasing eyes. "How long did you stay? After I fell asleep."

He hesitated. "I left around five."

"You stayed all night." She glanced up at him. Then away. "I always wondered."

"You looked so sad. So vulnerable, even while you were asleep." He placed a finger under her chin and lifted until her gaze met his. "I couldn't bear to leave you."

"Thank you. For staying with me. For letting me cry on your shoulder." She dropped her gaze. "It was selfish of me to cry, you know."

"Don't say tha—"

She cut him off. "I wasn't crying for Kevin. That's so awful of me to say, but it's true. He'd been cheating on me. Our marriage was over even before he died. So I was crying for me. I didn't know what would happen. How Mom and Dad would feel. What if they didn't love me anymore since Kevin was gone?" Her voice caught.

She brushed a tear off her cheek with her free hand. "Even before he died, I wondered what would happen. Obviously Kevin didn't love me anymore. I didn't care so much about my marriage ending, it had been over for a long time, but I did care about losing Mom and Dad. And Lauren. The only real family I'd ever known."

She took a deep breath and pulled her hand from his. He seemed reluctant to let her go. She scrubbed her face with her hands. "Oh crap. Not again. This is the second time this week I've cried on you."

"I don't mind."

She shook her head and tried for a lighter tone.

"Well I do. Maybe we shouldn't make a habit of sitting out at this table together. I go to pieces every time we do."

"Okay." He smiled. "Next time I'll shower before we eat so I won't feel so bad about sitting on your furniture."

****

"Hi, Erika. It's Lauren. I need a huge favor."

"What's up?" Erika tucked the phone between her shoulder and her ear so she could continue putting the dishes away.

"I have to head out of town earlier than I expected. Jim's meeting got changed, and I wondered if you could watch the girls."

"I'd love to." She stifled a yawn.

"Are you sure? You sound tired. I don't want to impose, but Mom and Dad are still at work."

"It's not a problem," she said, although Lauren had been right. Erika was tired. Talking to Chase about spending the night in his arms hadn't stopped the dreams. If anything, they were more vivid than ever. Her nights hadn't been very restful lately. The thought of him triggered something in her mind. "Wouldn't Chase want to take the girls?"

"I can't get hold of him." The usual touch of annoyance laced Lauren's voice as she spoke of her ex-husband. "His phone goes straight to voicemail. He must be in a dead zone with his cell. I'll leave a message letting him know he can pick up the girls at your place. Jim and I will drop them off on our way to the airport."

Good thing Chase wasn't working there today. Then again, if he had been, Lauren probably would have been able to get a hold of him. "Sounds like a plan."

"Thanks. You're a lifesaver. The girls will be so excited."

"See you in a bit."

Within the hour her doorbell rang. The girls launched themselves at her as soon as she opened the door.

"Hi, Aunt Erika."

"Okay," Lauren said. "Your father will come to get you after work. Be good for Aunt Erika."

"We will," they chorused.

Lauren turned to go. "Thanks again. I'm not sure when Chase will be here."

"Whenever is fine. We'll find plenty to do until he gets here." Her gaze fell on the bright green permit hanging in the window by the door. Would Lauren notice it? Would she ask about the work going on?

Thankfully, the other woman seemed preoccupied. She glanced out toward the street. "I've got to run. Jim is waiting in the car. Bye, sweeties. I'll see you on Monday."

"Bye, Mommy."

"Bye."

The door had no sooner closed behind their mother when the girls turned chocolate brown eyes to Erika. Although not identical, they looked so much like Chase it made her heart skip a beat.

"Can we watch *Little Mermaid*?"

"Can we have hotdogs?"

The excited voices tumbled over one another as they danced around her.

"Yes and yes." She laughed at their exuberance.

"But let's save those for later. I thought we'd go outside since it's so nice today." The day was far less humid than it had been in the last few weeks, leaving a pleasantly warm summer day.

"What are we gonna do outside?" Steph asked.

"Would you like to do some painting?"

"Cool," Sami said.

"Okay, let's get some lemonade, and then we'll gather our supplies and head out."

The afternoon passed in a whirl of activity. Before they knew it, suppertime arrived. Erika was filling a pot with water to cook the hotdogs when the doorbell pealed.

"Daddy's home!" Steph and Sami shrieked in chorus and raced for the foyer.

Erika wiped her hands on a dishtowel, and then followed. She opened the front door, but before Chase could step inside, two dark-haired tornadoes launched themselves at him. Erika wouldn't let herself dwell on the scene of domestic bliss that sprang to mind at the girls' words and actions. Chase hunkered down and gathered his daughters close to his heart, shutting his eyes for a moment as if savoring the contact.

They remained in his arms as he rose and then kissed each in turn. "I missed you."

"We missed you, too." Sami cuddled into his neck.

"You forgot to kiss Aunt Erika," Steph said.

Erika's startled gaze flew to Chase's. The brown orbs danced with laughter and mischief.

"So I did." He leaned toward her.

Expecting to feel the brush of his lips against her cheek, she started when he touched his mouth to hers in a soft kiss. The brief contact sent a shock of awareness through her. For a moment she could only stare. His gesture had been purely innocent, but her nerves zinged and her heart raced. A warm flush spread through her.

Her gaze locked with Chase's. For endless heartbeats she stared into the deep mocha of his eyes. Could he hear the rapid thumps against her ribs?

"Daddy, I'm hungry." Sami placed a small hand on either side of Chase's face and turned it toward her, breaking the intense stare.

Erika gave herself a mental shake. "We were about to eat. Care to join us for a hotdog?" The simple question gave no outward sign of the rapid beating of her heart. She congratulated herself on the casual tone of her voice.

"Ah, the four-year-old's gourmet food of choice. Sounds good to me." Chase set the girls on the floor. "Can we help?"

"Tell you what." Erika said. "Why don't you show your daddy the pictures you painted for him, and I'll finish up in the kitchen."

"C'mon, Daddy." Steph grabbed one of Chase's hands. Sami clutched the other. They dragged him into the living room.

He glanced over his shoulder as the twins led him away. "You sure you don't need any help?"

"I'm good. You sit with your girls." Erika escaped to the kitchen, trying not to think about the brush of his lips against hers. It didn't mean anything. Friends greeted each other with a kiss all the time. So why was her heartbeat only beginning to slow?

The patter of small feet, followed by the heavier tread of boots alerted her to the trio's presence.

"I can grill those if you want."

She glanced over her shoulder. "Isn't that too much trouble? I was just going to cook them on the stove."

"It's no trouble at all. And it's not summer until you've had a perfectly grilled hot dog. Steaming on the inside, with just a touch of black char on the outside."

Her mouth watered. "Okay, your way sounds much better than boiled on the stove." She tossed him the package of hotdogs, which he caught in one hand. "You get started on those then, and I'll get the buns and condiments ready."

"Got it." However, before he made it to the door, his cell phone rang. He pulled it from the holder on his belt and peered at the screen. "I need to answer this. I'll be right out."

Erika chewed a fingernail. What could possibly take him away this time? The girls were already here. Forcing the unease aside, she put buns, ketchup, and mustard on a tray, then distributed plates and napkins to Sami and Steph. They followed her out the back door onto the patio.

"I love being with Daddy," Sami said.

"When Mommy goes on vacation with Jim we're gonna stay with Daddy for a whole week," Steph announced.

Another trip? Lauren must be getting really serious about Jim. What did Chase think about the relationship? He certainly wouldn't like sharing his daughters with another man.

"That's great," Erika said. "I'm sure you'll have lots of fun."

"I wish we could stay with Daddy all the time," Sami added wistfully.

The screen door slid smoothly in its track and

Chase stepped out onto the patio.

"Everything okay?" Erika couldn't help but ask.

"Yep. Just a customer with a question."

After pressing the button to light the grill, he turned to the girls and rubbed his hands together. "Who wants to play football while the grill heats?"

"Me!"

"Me, too!"

"Where did you find a football?" Erika asked. The profound relief that he wasn't leaving filled her with an almost giddy elation.

Chase grinned. "My truck."

"I want Aunt Erika on my team," Steph called.

"No fair," Sami said. Her lower lip protruded.

"What am I, chopped liver?" Chase groused, a good-natured grin on his face.

"Liver?"

"Eeuwwwwwww."

Chase's chuckles blended with Erika's laughter. "Just a saying, moppets." He ruffled their hair. "Now, what are we going to do about those teams?" He looked thoughtful. Then his face brightened. "I know. We'll flip for it."

He grabbed Sami and flipped her upside down over his arm. Shrieking with delight, she completed a full circle, using Chase's strong arms like a jungle gym. Obviously the routine had been performed before. Steph immediately copied the procedure after her sister.

Erika envied the intimate family scene. What would it be like if she and Kevin had had children? Maybe things would have been different. Maybe he wouldn't have spent so much time away, occupied with other things. Other women. Would children have kept him at home? Or made things worse?

She'd always wanted children. It had been a shock when she found out only after she married Kevin he didn't want to have kids. It shocked her even more to discover the image in her mind now didn't show her and Kevin with children, but her and Chase and the twins. As a family.

She swallowed to ease the sudden dryness in her throat.

The girls were still laughing dizzily when Chase said, "Well, that was fun, but it didn't solve anything. Tell you what, Steph, you start with me and Sami with Aunt Erika. We'll switch at halftime."

A chorus of agreement met his proposal.

So while the grill heated, the players engaged in a frenzied game of football. Taking turns, Erika or Chase passed the ball to their respective twin, who ran with the ball until the opposing adult grabbed her with a tickling tackle. Halftime occurred when Chase put the hotdogs on the grill, and then play resumed with new teams.

After a few more throws, Steph grew bored. "You run with the ball now," she told Erika. So Erika ran and allowed herself to be tackled by a giggling Sami.

"Now it's my turn to tackle Daddy." Steph threw herself at his feet as he ran. To avoid stepping on her, Chase veered, and although he hadn't been running fast, his momentum, along with the sharp turn brought him crashing into Erika.

The breath whooshed out of her lungs as his arms closed around her. He twisted as they tumbled to the ground to take the brunt of the fall upon himself.

"Aunt Erika tackled Daddy!" Steph clapped her

hands.

The childish delight in the words barely registered. Erika sprawled full length over an extremely male body. Chase's heart thudded beneath hers as his chest heaved. The hair on his legs tickled the smooth skin of her own. The soft curves of her body pressed against firm muscles.

The awareness in his dark eyes mirrored the same things. She couldn't tear her gaze away from his intense stare. His arms tightened around her as his gaze moved from hers to focus on her mouth. Without conscious thought, her lips parted. His breath whispered over her face as his raised.

"Daddy, the hot dogs are on fire!"

Chapter Five

Despite being hyper-aware of the man who sat across the table, Erika thoroughly enjoyed dinner. The girls' laughter dominated the conversation as they filled Chase in on what they'd done during the day. The hotdogs, a new batch grilled to perfection after the first ones burned, were consumed long before the chattering girls ran out of things to talk about.

At last Chase pushed back his chair and tossed his paper napkin on the table. Erika rose. "Let me get this stuff out of the way."

"Why don't you two help Aunt Erika clean up, and then we need to hit the road."

Disappointment stabbed through her. The accompanying groans of the twins echoed the emotion.

"But we didn't get to watch *Little Mermaid*," Steph said.

"You're more than welcome to stay and watch," Erika offered before she could stop herself.

Chase's gaze came to rest on her. Something in his eyes unnerved her, as if he sensed the underlying reason behind her offer. She didn't want to let him go yet.

"Unless you have other plans," she added.

"Please, Daddy?"

"Pleeeze?"

Chase sought Erika's gaze once again. "Are you sure? They've seen it a million times. They'll survive not watching it tonight."

"I'd love to have them stay." Erika kept her tone casual and focused on the children. "I didn't have any plans tonight anyway."

He studied her. Finally, he nodded. "Okay, then. We'll stay." A chorus of cheers met Chase's statement.

He rose. "Would you mind if I take a quick shower first? I don't want to sit on your living room furniture in these clothes." He swept a hand in front of himself, drawing attention not only to the evidence of a day's hard work splattered on the T-shirt, but to the toned and muscled physique beneath as well.

Heat suffused her face as she imagined Chase undressing in her small bathroom. Would the rest of his body be tanned like his arms and face? Or would areas usually hidden from other's eyes be pale? Where would the tan line begin? End? "Th-that's fine. Let me get you a towel." Glad for a task to keep her mind off the erotic images flitting through her brain, Erika hurried into the house. When she returned to the kitchen, Chase and the girls had cleared the table, and the plates had been loaded into the dishwasher.

"Thanks," she said. "You didn't have to do that."

"It was the least we could do." He flashed his charming smile.

She swallowed. "You can use the bathroom down here. I put a towel on the counter for you."

"Perfect. Thanks. Tell you what, I'll run out to the truck and grab a change of clothes and then shower. Why don't you ladies start the movie, and I'll join you when I'm done."

"Okay." Steph grabbed one of Erika's hands and Sami copied by taking the other. "C'mon, let's watch."

So Erika settled onto the couch with the girls while Chase cleaned up and changed. She soon found the antics of the Little Mermaid and her seagoing friends were no match for the sight of Chase returning to the living room after his shower. His dark hair curled damply where it touched the edge of a crisp, clean T-shirt. Khaki cargo shorts hugged his hips. His feet were bare.

Bringing her gaze slowly back up over the black shirt stretched tight across his chest, her stare collided with his. Her tongue darted out to lick her parched lips, and her pulse quickened as his eyes tracked the gesture. When they returned to hers, the dark irises stole her breath. For endless moments they stared at one another.

"This is my favorite part." Steph's excited voice broke the tension.

After the space of another heartbeat, Chase pulled his gaze from Erika's, and her breath escaped in a rush. He made himself comfortable on the other couch by turning sideways and draping his long legs over the arm. Sami crawled over to cuddle in his arms. For a moment, Erika envied the little girl. She wanted to be the one curled up with Chase. But then Steph scooted over to settle next to her, and she made a concerted effort to watch the movie.

By keeping her eyes riveted on the TV screen she forced herself to focus on the cartoon, rather than the presence of the man sprawled on the sofa across the room. About halfway through the movie, she got up to pop a bag of popcorn in the microwave. When she returned, Steph and Sami had switched places.

"I wanna sit with you now," Sami whispered as Erika sat down again.

"I'm glad." Erika squeezed the girl close. Over the top of the dark head, she caught Chase's gaze. He winked. She smiled back utterly content with the cozy family scene playing out in her living room.

Chase rose to refill his beverage, and she caught the clean, soap smell of him as he passed by. Her position on the couch gave her the perfect vantage point to view his strong legs as they carried him out of the room. His hip-hugging shorts distracted her once again from the movie. Hands down he was the sexiest man she had ever met.

She shook her head in a forcible attempt to rein in her inappropriate thoughts. She shouldn't be thinking those things about him. She was his daughters' aunt. His ex-wife's sister-in-law. But she had a hard time remembering those details when he returned. Her gaze kept straying to where he reclined.

His glance met hers when the small, red crab on the TV screen began to sing. As soon as he launched into his song, Erika's willpower slipped away. As the crustacean told the cartoon prince to kiss the girl, Chase's gaze remained fixed on hers. His eyes reflected the words of the song. He wanted to kiss her.

She swallowed. Or tried to. Her throat was too dry to manage the reflexive movement. Because, like the girl in the movie, she wanted him to kiss her, too. The rest of the room faded until the world had narrowed to those warm, brown eyes focused intently on her. She could easily drown in their melting heat.

A childish giggle broke the sensual haze. "Daddy, they fell in the water."

Erika forced her gaze away from Chase. A quick dunk in a cold lake wouldn't be such a bad idea.

She shook off the feeling, and once again attempted to concentrate on the movie. Soon the girls drifted off and, eager for something to do to keep her mind off forbidden topics, she rose to gather the remains of their snack. She reached for the empty popcorn bowl as Chase did the same. Her hand brushed his, and she yanked it away as if burned.

"Erika." Her name came out soft. Husky. Never before had it sounded so intimate on a man's lips.

"I need to get this cleaned up." She fled to the kitchen.

She stood by the sink, the snack dishes forgotten. Her hands gripped the edge of the granite so hard her knuckles turned white.

The soft pad of Chase's bare feet announced his arrival a moment before his hands came to rest on her shoulders. She flinched.

"Erika." How easily she could get used to him saying her name just like that. As though velvet secrets hid in the simple syllables. She shivered under his touch. "What are you thinking?"

As if he didn't know. She shook her head, unable to speak, or unwilling to voice her thoughts aloud.

With gentle hands he turned her to face him. "Look at me." He lifted her chin with a finger.

She tried to tear her gaze from his, but the intensity in the dark depths of his eyes made the task impossible. The silent communication spoke to her soul in a way nothing ever had before.

"It's okay." His breath fanned across her face.

No, it's not, she wanted to say, but the words wouldn't come.

His hand brushed the side of her face, then

threaded in her hair, cupping the back of her head. All the while his eyes studied her. Spoke to her. Disarmed her. The strong fingers at her nape drew her face upward as his descended.

"Please." The word was both plea and prayer. Her pulse fluttered in an erratic rhythm. Her hands rose to clasp his upper arms. The muscles flexed slightly as he applied pressure to the back of her head.

Then his mouth covered hers. Heat coursed through her and consumed her. The light brush of his lips against hers earlier had left her shaken. Now the firm urgency of his mouth sent an earthquake-like jolt through her.

His lips parted over hers, and the kiss became wetter, hotter. When she shuddered, he groaned deep in his throat and gathered her close, pulling her against his chest. The thundering beat of his heart matched the quick tripping of her own.

She gasped, and Chase took the opportunity to draw his mouth from hers for an instant. "You taste like popcorn," he teased. But when he hurried his lips back to hers, there was nothing lighthearted about the mind-scrambling kiss. His masterful mouth brushed, stroked, and devoured hers.

Lost in the sensual haze, she barely heard the voice from the living room.

Chase pulled his mouth from hers. "I'm here, Sami," he said in response to the little girl's sleepy call. "I'll be right there."

With her face buried in his neck, the vibration of his words hummed against her cheek. She marveled at the evenness of his voice. If she had needed to speak right then only squeaky syllables would have emerged.

The pulse racing in Chase's throat gradually returned to a normal rhythm. When her heart no longer pounded in her chest, she took a deep breath, inhaling the scent of her soap on his heated skin. The erotic combination sent her pulse skittering again.

She pulled away, unable to look at him. He let her go. She sensed his reluctance. His arms dropped to his sides. "I have to go to Sami."

She nodded. As soon as he left, she raised a trembling hand to her lips. They were still wet from his kiss. How far would they have gone if Sami hadn't interrupted them? Thank God for four-year-old chaperones.

She smoothed her hair as she summoned the courage to return to the other room. She had to get a grip on her emotions. They weren't the first two people to ever kiss. People kissed all the time. But did they kiss their brothers-in-law?

In the living room Chase was gathering the twins' belongings. Both girls lay on the couch half-asleep. Erika's gaze met his. Although no words were said, his spoke volumes. It caressed her face, coming to rest on her still moist lips. Her pulse quickened, and the blood in her veins grew warm as it lingered.

Finally he cleared his throat, breaking the loud silence. "I have to get the girls home to bed."

What would it be like to go to bed with Chase? She'd done it a hundred times in her dreams. What would it be like for real? She pushed the teasing, tempting fantasy away and nodded. "They…they look beat."

"Thanks for watching them until I could get here."

"It was my pleasure."

"They had a good time."

"So did I." She cringed at the inane small talk.

"Would you mind carrying Sami to the truck?" He lifted Steph in his strong arms. The little girl murmured something and cuddled sleepily against his chest.

Erika scooped Sami from the couch and followed Chase out the front door. His truck sat at the curb. He set Steph in the extended cab with gentle care, and then buckled her into a booster seat. He walked around to the other side of the truck, took the sleeping girl from Erika's arms, and buckled her in as well.

Not sure what to do with her empty hands, and aching to touch Chase again, Erika jammed them into her back pockets.

He shut the door with a soft thump, and then turned toward her. Once again their eyes met. Held. Communicated. She shivered at the raw hunger in his gaze. Did hers reflect the same gnawing emotion?

"Good night." He leaned down to brush a kiss, more air than substance, across her lips. It didn't lessen the impact one iota.

Long after his truck pulled out of the driveway and disappeared down the street, she stood with her fingers pressed to her mouth. Her world had not only spun out of control tonight, but had tilted right off its axis. She and Chase had crossed a line, and God help her, even if she'd been able to, she wouldn't go back and change a single moment.

****

Later, Chase lay awake, his mind and body too wound up to sleep. In his head he kept hearing Sami say she wished she could live with him all the time. He wanted that, too. It tortured him to only see the girls on the weekends. Even the simple act of tucking them into bed those few nights brought a poignant reminder of the day to day things he missed out on.

All too soon, it would be Sunday night again, and he'd need to take them back to Lauren's. Even the thought of leaving them brought an ache to his heart.

He wanted to be more than a see-you-on-the-weekends dad. The weekends flew by much too quickly. He never had enough time to do all of the things he wanted to with the girls. The pleasure of watching a movie with them and hearing their childish giggles was bittersweet, because he didn't get to do it everyday.

Tonight had been fun. Having dinner with Erika. Playing football. The movie.

Of course the memory of Erika's body sprawled over his during the football game contributed to his insomnia as well. How could he sleep with his body aware, aroused, and aching in every pore?

The explicit details of their kiss were etched into his soul. The salty taste of popcorn on her lips. The strawberry scent of her shampoo. The way he'd moaned a little in the back of her throat when he deepened the kiss. How her hands had clutched him closer.

He screwed his eyes shut, but it only made the memories more vivid. The details sharper. He rolled to his side and buried his face in the pillow.

The night stretched endlessly before him.

****

"How did things go with Chase the other night?"

Erika's startled gaze flew to her sister-in-law. Her hand paused in the act of cutting the celery in front of her. "What?" For a moment panic filled her. How could

Lauren know about the kiss? She couldn't. Erika inhaled through her nostrils to calm her racing pulse.

"He got to you at a decent hour, right? Sometimes when he works he loses all track of time."

"Oh." *Breathe*, Erika reminded herself as she resumed chopping. "He wasn't late at all. He got there right before dinner."

"Oh, good. Then you had plenty of time to yourself after they left." Lauren reached for another carrot.

Erika concentrated on the celery before her. Had the girls mentioned staying at her house for dinner? Watching the movie? Heat suffused her face at the memory of what the movie had led to with Chase. She swallowed to ease the nervous tightening in her throat. She didn't want to lie to Lauren. Of course she didn't want to tell her the whole truth either.

"Actually, we were about to sit down and eat, so the girls and Chase stayed for dinner and…and to watch a movie." She didn't look at Lauren as she spoke. Would the other woman hear the slight shake in her voice?

"Oh, Erika. I'm so sorry."

Now Erika glanced up. "What for?" Shouldn't she be the sorry one? For kissing Lauren's ex-husband.

"I didn't mean for the girls to disrupt your whole night."

Erika waved the knife in her hand. "It wasn't a disruption. Really. I had…fun." Too much fun as it turned out.

"Well, at any rate. Thanks again. I'm sure you had fun with the girls, but I didn't mean to subject you to Chase's company for the evening." The tone of her voice made it evident how *she* felt about Chase's company.

"Really. It wasn't a problem. I-I didn't mind." What would Lauren say if she found out Erika and Chase had spent a lot of evenings together the past few weeks while he'd been working at her house? She changed the subject. "How was your trip? Did you have a good time with Jim in D.C.?"

"Fabulous." Lauren looked up. Her eyes sparkled. "I really like him. In fact, I'm pretty sure I'm in love with him."

"That's wonderful." Erika was truly happy for her sister-in-law.

"Although, there's one thing not so great. There's a chance Jim is going to be transferred to Washington."

"Oh no. How soon?"

"Within the next year or two." She shook her head. "I don't know how we could make it work. Packing up and moving out there isn't as easy as it seems. I mean, Chase would have a fit if I even mentioned it."

Erika grimaced. Talk about an understatement. She couldn't begin to imagine his reaction if Lauren told him she was moving with the girls. Would their custody agreement even allow her to move halfway across the country?

"What's Chase having a fit about this time?" Louise asked as she walked into the kitchen.

Lauren shook her head at Erika and mouthed, "Don't say anything."

Erika nodded. Having lost her only son a year ago, Louise wouldn't take the news of her daughter moving away very well.

Lauren turned to her mother. "Oh, the usual." She scooped her pile of carrots into the pot sitting on the table. "What else goes into this soup?"

"If Erika's all set with the celery?"

Erika scraped the pile of vegetables from the cutting board into the pot.

"Great. The chicken's ready. Then we'll add the noodles to the broth and be good to go." Louise finished preparing the soup, adjusted the burner, and left it on the stove to simmer. She opened a cabinet to pull out some dishes. She turned to Lauren. "Is Jim coming for dinner?"

Lauren shook her head. "Not tonight. He's teaching a seminar at the community college. He'll probably come over to my place when he's done."

"You two sure are spending a lot of time together lately. Is it getting serious?" A hopeful note crept into Louise's tone.

Lauren smiled. Her expression softened. "I think it may be."

"How wonderful."

"I think so. He makes me really happy." Contentment laced her sigh. "How's your love life these days?"

Erika scrambled to keep up with the change of topic. "What?"

"Lauren, really," Louise admonished. "It's much too early for Erika to think about dating. Kevin's been gone less than a year, rest his soul." She crossed herself.

Erika's pulse raced as guilt zeroed in on her heart. No, she wasn't dating anyone, but she had kissed someone. She'd kissed Chase. Her stomach knotted.

"Oh, Mom, please. It's been long enough. Jim works with this really great guy. He would be perfect for you," Lauren said to Erika.

"Lauren!" Shock and dismay blended in Louise's voice. "How could you? Have you forgotten your brother so soon?" She sat at the table. Tears formed in the corners of her eyes.

Erika laid a comforting hand on Louise's shoulder, hoping the older woman couldn't feel her trembling. "Thanks, but I don't think so," she said to Lauren.

Lauren leaned down to give her mother a quick squeeze. "I'm sorry, Mom. Of course I haven't forgotten Kevin."

"I know you haven't." Louise rose from the chair. "It's too soon for Erika, don't you think?"

"Sure," Lauren said.

Erika mumbled an incoherent reply. Her heart pounded and her head spun, making her dizzy. How could she have let herself get so carried away with Chase? He'd kissed her. Worse, she'd kissed him back. Her body flushed from the memory of his mouth on hers. And, God help her, she wanted to do it again.

She looked at her mother-in-law's stricken face. The guilt squeezed tighter around her heart.

Louise glanced over at Erika. "It's too soon," she repeated.

Erika nodded. What could she say? Louise didn't know the truth about her marriage. She didn't know it had been over long before Kevin's death. Erika vowed she never would.

"You know I still think of you as a daughter. You'll always be a part of this family."

Erika swallowed the lump in her throat. Would Louise feel the same way if she found out about Erika and Chase?

****

Later, Erika walked into her house and tossed her purse on the table with a sigh. Dinner with the family had been...difficult. Keeping the memory of Chase's kiss at bay. Listening to Lauren's usual disparaging comments. Louise's response when Lauren mentioned setting Erika up on a date.

The thoughts ran through her mind in a never-ending loop, making her head throb. She rubbed her temples. A glance at the clock in the entryway showed it was later than she thought.

Without bothering to turn on the lights, she headed up the stairs. One step into the bathroom her foot splashed into a puddle of water. "What the hell?"

From the safety of the hall, she reached around the corner to flip on the light. A steady trickle of water poured from behind the pedestal sink.

"Damn." She sloshed over the sodden throw rug covering the black and white patterned tile floor to peer behind the base. Water dripped from a seam in the pipes. With a sigh dredged from the soles of her feet, she kneeled in the wet to twist the valve. It came off in her hand. The trickle became a stream. "Double damn."

She hurried to the kitchen to retrieve the bucket from under the sink. Returning to the bathroom she placed it under the pipe. Perched on the edge of the claw foot tub, she chewed a fingernail and surveyed the rapid rate at which the bucket filled. What now?

She needed help. After emptying the bucket into the tub, she replaced it beneath the leak, then grabbed the cordless phone from the bedroom. Chase's deep voice answered on the second ring.

"Hi, it's Erika."

"Hi." If her late night call surprised him, his tone didn't show it.

"Um, I hate to bother you, but my bathroom sink is leaking and—"

"I'll be right over."

"Oh, no, I don't need you to come over. I don't know where the main shut off is," Erika admitted.

"Shut it off at the back of the sink."

"I tried that, but the knob came off in my hand."

Chase cursed, echoing Erika's earlier appraisal of the situation. "How bad is it?"

Taking the phone with her, she padded to the bathroom to survey the damage. "Well, I emptied the bucket under the sink right before I called you, and it's nearly full again."

"That's flowing pretty fast." His voice didn't sound encouraging.

Duh. "Like I said, I need to know where the main valve is. I'll call a plumber in the morning."

"I'll be over as soon as I can. Keep bailing." He hung up before she could protest again.

By the time Chase arrived she'd emptied the bucket too many times to count. The stream had become a river.

"You didn't need to come over. I hate to bother you."

"It's no bother. And maybe I can fix it for you so you don't need to call a plumber."

But after assessing the situation, Chase emerged from the bathroom, a grim look on his face. "It's worse than I thought. The pipe's rusted through. I can't stop the water flow without replacing the entire section. I don't have the parts with me, and," he glanced down at his watch, "I don't think we'll find any stores open at this hour. We'll have to shut off the water and deal with it in the morning."

Erika refrained from pointing out that had been her plan all along.

Chase went down to the basement, but returned shortly. "Okay all set. Why don't you throw whatever you'll need for tonight in a bag and we can hit the road."

"Great. Thanks, I'll—" She stopped as his words registered. "Wait. What?"

He raised a quizzical eyebrow. "Don't you want a change of clothes for the morning at least?"

She frowned up at him. "I'm not going anywhere."

"You can't stay here. You don't have any running water. I shut everything off. You can stay with me."

The memory of his warm, moist kiss swept through her and left her dizzy. Her pulse raced as if his lips were on hers again. An unexpected image, straight from one of her dreams, of the two of them tangled in the sheets of Chase's bed sprang into her mind. She blushed and looked away. "I don't think that's such a good idea."

"Why not? You need a place to stay. I have a pullout couch. Seems like a simple solution to me." He folded his arms across his chest.

She shook her head. If she spent the night at his house she'd want so much more than a spare bed. She'd want to live out her dreams. And it scared her.

"Is it because I kissed you?"

She started at the blunt question. Had he read her thoughts? "No. Yes. I don't know." The kiss in her kitchen wasn't the issue. Not really. Her apprehension stemmed mostly from her desperate need to be kissed by him again.

Chase's eyes filled with some indefinable emotion. "Are you upset I kissed you?" His even tone gave no hint to his thoughts.

Unable to respond, she shook her head in a helpless gesture. How could she explain it to him? She couldn't explain it to herself. Part of her *was* upset he'd kissed her. Her conscience flooded with guilt every time she thought of her family. But other parts of her still tingled and grew warm at the memory of his talented lips brushing over hers.

He stepped closer, forcing her to tilt her head up to look at him, and raised a hand to trace a finger down the side of her face. A searing path of heat followed in the wake of his light touch. Conversely, she shivered.

His lips quirked. "If I promise not to kiss you again, will you spend the night with me?"

Chapter Six

In spite of herself, Erika smiled at the contradictory words. "It's not that. Well, not entirely."

"Then what?"

"What if my family finds out?" She voiced one of her fears, not sure if it was the more prevalent one or not.

Chase went very still. He didn't say anything for long moments. Finally he spoke. "That's what you're worried about?"

She nodded. That amongst other things. Like not being able to stop herself from slipping into his bed and living out one of her dreams.

The drip of the remaining water in the pipes carried easily in the silence as he studied her. "Well, we would be the only ones who will know you'll be at my place. And if you don't tell anyone, and I don't tell anyone, then no one will find out. Right?"

"I suppose." The words came out slowly, her voice hesitant with reluctance.

"Great. It's settled then. Grab your things."

"I really don't think this is a good idea." She nibbled on a fingernail. "Maybe you can turn the water on, and I can keep bailing."

"All night? I don't think so. You won't get any sleep." He paused. "Would you rather go to a hotel?"

Oooh, hotel sex? She ignored the naughty voice in

her head. Chase hadn't meant he'd go to the hotel with her. Had he?

No, of course not.

Staying at a hotel would be another hit to her already tight budget. She'd rather not spend the money, especially with a plumbing bill on the way. Even if Chase could fix the problem, she still needed to pay for the parts. Staying at his house would be free.

Except for the emotional price.

As if sensing her indecision, he turned the full force of his persuasive eyes on her. "Come on, please. I promise no one will find out. You look dead on your feet. You need to get some sleep."

Hearing the words out loud intensified the bone-weary tiredness weighing her down. Unable to resist the pull of his compelling gaze, but against her better judgment, she gave in. "Okay. Give me a few minutes to get ready."

"Take your time. I'll wait downstairs."

After Chase's footsteps had retreated down the stairs, she sagged against the wall. Was she playing with fire? His mere presence in her life these past few weeks had left her with erotic dreams and gnawing guilt. What would happen if she slept under the same roof, knowing he slumbered only down the hall?

And what if her family found out? Despite his assurances, a knot of apprehension tightened her stomach and sharpened the guilt.

She yawned then shook herself awake. She needed to get to sleep. Her steps dragged as she headed toward her bedroom to throw some things into an overnight bag.

The ride to Chase's home sped by, punctuated by

idle conversation and plans for fixing the plumbing the next day. Too soon they pulled up in front of the two-car garage facing the tree-lined street. He shut off the engine.

They sat in the sudden quiet. Tense seconds ticked by. Shadows darkened the nightscape outside the truck's windows.

"It's okay," he said at last.

Erika couldn't help but remember he'd spoken those exact words right before he kissed her the other night. Her emotions had been far from okay ever since. However, try as she might, she couldn't make herself regret those stolen moments in his arms. And as for the night's sleeping arrangements, it was too late to back out now.

"Sure." Erika opened the door and stepped down from the truck.

Inside the house, she fiddled with the strap of her bag as she glanced around the living room. Chase had decorated in natural tones. The furniture looked both stylish and comfortable. A brown sectional faced an entertainment center that held a flat-screen TV and a stereo system. Framed photographs of the twins filled the mantel above the fireplace. Off to one side sat a recliner. Bookshelves lined the far wall.

She walked over to take a closer look. Mysteries and thrillers jammed the shelves, mixed with a variety of children's books. Her fingers fluttered over the spines.

"I'll take the sofa. You can sleep in my room."

Erika jumped. Her nerves skittered then stretched tight. She turned. He stood next to the couch, a pillow and a blanket in his arms.

She shook her head. No way. Sleeping in the same house would be bad enough. Sleeping in his bed was out of the question. "No, I'll be fine out here."

He opened his mouth.

"Don't argue with me," she warned.

He sighed. "I wouldn't think of it. Here." He handed her the linens.

"Thanks." She tossed the blanket and pillow on the couch. He moved toward her. She froze then took a small step back.

His eyes tracked the movement before narrowing. "I'll open the bed for you."

"Don't bother. I'll sleep on it the way it is."

"Erika."

"Really. It'll be fine. I don't want you to go to any trouble." She didn't plan on getting much sleep anyway with him right down the hall. Tempting her. Combined with the guilt eating at her, she'd be awake most of the night. "I-I appreciate you letting me stay here."

"No problem." He inclined his head toward a doorway on the far side of the room. "There's a bathroom down the hall."

"Thanks."

He headed in the direction he'd indicated. "Good-night," he said over his shoulder.

After he'd gone, Erika sank onto the sofa and released the breath she'd been holding. She buried her face in her hands. Had she lost her mind? What was she doing? What was she thinking? Why was she here, risking everything?

Bad enough she'd hired Chase to work for her. Worse, she'd kissed him. Now she'd topped it all off with spending the night at his house. Her common sense had not only flown out the window, it had disappeared entirely.

Normally, she considered herself a rational, levelheaded woman. But apparently if it involved Chase, she turned into a flighty, hormone-riddled idiot.

****

Chase turned in the doorway. Erika's dejected pose tugged at his heart. She hadn't wanted to come tonight. What made her so reluctant? Fear of Lauren's family finding out, or, although she denied it, regret over their kiss?

Either option made him feel like a jerk. Even though he didn't put much stock in what the Garretts thought about him, Erika did care. They meant everything to her. Having to lie to them must be tearing her up inside. Keeping secrets, especially from those you loved, was hard.

She had too many she carried around.

And now he'd added to the burden—first by convincing her to hire him, and again by talking her into spending the night at his house.

Not to mention their kiss. Since that night in her kitchen, the memory had taunted him. Kept him awake at night wanting to kiss her again. To take the kiss further.

Which he had no right to do, for many reasons. Not the least of which being he had nothing to offer in return. He didn't want to be in a relationship. He didn't need anyone else in his life. He had his daughters. His job kept him busy. He didn't have time for all the rigmarole dating involved.

Hey, Erika, how about a quick roll in the hay? wasn't going to cut it.

She deserved more. Someone who would treat her as if she were the most special person in the world. A woman like Erika, who was kind and compassionate and selfless, should have a man fall in love with her. Marry her.

He had no intention of getting married again. Once had been one time too many.

****

Erika lay awake in the dark and listened to the sounds of Chase's house. A clock ticked in the kitchen. The whoosh of the air conditioner as it kicked on. The slight squeak of mattress springs as he got into bed.

Her body vibrated with awareness. Chase slept right down the hall. Did he sleep in pajamas? Boxers? Nothing at all? The urge to find out proved almost impossible to ignore.

What would he do if she padded down the hall into his room? Told him about her dreams. Asked him to make them come true. She clenched her fists so tightly the nails dug into her palms. The pain brought her to her senses.

She rolled to her side and buried her face in the pillow. His woodsy scent clung to the blanket covering her. She inhaled and imagined being wrapped in his arms instead of the soft cotton.

Her dreams would be explicit tonight.

The next morning Erika woke to the smell of frying bacon, surprised she'd fallen asleep at all. The aching want permeating her body had kept her awake most of the night. As she'd known it would.

She sat up and stretched in an attempt to coax tightened muscles to relax. The couch hadn't been unbearable, but definitely not as comfortable as the king-sized mattress at home.

From the kitchen came the quiet clatter of pots and pans. Chase. She swallowed to ease the dryness in her throat. They'd done wildly sexy things in her dreams last night. How could she face him this morning?

Putting off the inevitable for a few moments, she grabbed her makeup bag and scurried down the hall to the bathroom. Condensation dripped in rivulets down the mirror. The scent of Chase's soap lingered. A towel hung on a hook on the back of the door. Unable to stop herself, she touched the damp terrycloth he'd used to absorb the water from his naked body. Her grip tightened, and the fabric twisted in her fingers.

She swallowed and forced her hold to relax. After brushing her teeth and splashing cold water on her face, her pulse calmed. She applied mascara to her lashes and liner to her eyes, but didn't bother with blush. Chase's nearness ensured her cheeks never lost a flushed glow. The familiar and simple task of smoothing her curls into a ponytail helped her gather almost enough courage to face him.

Almost. Her stomach somersaulted. Her hand trembled as she tucked a lock of hair behind her ear. She took a deep breath. Hiding in the bathroom wasn't an option.

In the kitchen Chase stood at the stove, tending a pan of scrambled eggs. On one of the other burners, bacon popped and sizzled in a frying pan. He sported a casual T-shirt and wind pants. His feet were bare. As if sensing her presence, he turned and offered a smile. "Good morning."

"Morning." She avoided looking directly at him. Remnants of last night's dream teased her. Here, standing in his kitchen, the images were more brilliant. Real.

"Breakfast will be ready in a minute. Do you want some coffee?"

"I'll get it." She needed the distraction. "You didn't have to make me breakfast." She poured herself a steaming mug from the pot on the counter. The carafe rattled against the sides of the maker as she replaced it. Clutching the cup to still the trembling in her hands, she took a seat at the small table in the corner and looked around.

The paintings the twins had done at her house hung on the refrigerator. Magnets featuring pictures of the girls and various cartoon characters adorned the rest of the appliance. White cabinets stood out against the burgundy walls. A large length of counter dominated the windowed wall. Like everything else in Chase's house, the kitchen was tastefully decorated, but functional. Comfortable.

She hadn't been able to think about her own kitchen in the same way since he had kissed her there. Her body heated from the memory of his touch whenever she walked into the room.

"All set." Chase placed a plate of bacon and eggs in front of her. "I hope you like scrambled."

"Scrambled is fine," she said. "I hope you didn't go to all this trouble for me."

"Nope." He joined her at the table. "I eat like this every morning."

Erika usually gulped a glass of juice and a couple of vitamins on her way out the door during the school year. In the summer she added a piece of toast and enjoyed her makeshift meal out on the patio.

"So after we're done here, we'll head over to the store and pick up the things we need to fix the pipe in your bathroom."

"I'm sure you have other things you need to do. I'll call a plumber when I get home."

"Don't be silly. I can fix it for you. I just have to rearrange a couple of things for today."

She shook her head. "I don't want to mess up your schedule. I should have brought my own car last night. At least you wouldn't have to drive me home first."

"I don't mind," he said after swallowing a bite of egg. "I enjoy your company." He leaned closer as if sharing a secret. "And I really enjoyed waking up with you here this morning."

Although several walls had separated them last night, his words filled the room with a sudden intimacy. Erika's blood raced, going hotter than the cup of coffee she had brought halfway to her mouth. Over the rim she gazed into eyes that she swore saw into her soul.

Chase finally broke the intense contact. "Finish your eggs," he said as if she were one of the girls. "They're getting cold."

She doubted it. His stare had generated enough heat to melt an iceberg. But she obediently finished the food in front of her.

After scraping his plate clean, Chase pushed back his chair and rose, the empty dish in his hand.

The phone rang and he grabbed it on his way to the sink. "Leave your plate on the table. I'll get it later," he told Erika before speaking into the receiver tucked against his ear. "Hello?" His brow furrowed. "What can I do for you?"

The change in his tone made Erika glance up.

He listened, his frown deepening. "No. You know the weekends are mine." He turned away and busied himself at the sink.

Erika's heart plummeted. Lauren.

"I'm not invited?" Chase asked.

They must be talking about the birthday party. She pushed back her chair, trying to make as little noise as possible.

"Then I'll bring them when I come." The patience in his tone sounded forced.

She reached around him to put her plate in the sink.

He put his finger over the mouthpiece. "You don't have to clean up. I'll take care of it," he said softly. "Yes, I heard you," he said into the phone. "I'll get them there whenever you want me to, but my daughters are going to be with me for the weekend. As always."

He listened. Then, "So you've said before. What time do you want me to bring them to your folks' house?"

Even through the tinny sound filtering through the phone, Erika sensed Lauren's displeasure.

"Lauren." A pause. "Noon. No problem." He replaced the receiver in its cradle then turned to face Erika.

She sat at the kitchen table and clutched the coffee mug. "Do you think Lauren knew I was here?" Panic made her heart beat faster.

"Of course not."

"But you were talking to me while you were on the phone with her." Her own fault. Why had she brought the plate to him at the sink?

Of all people to call. Lauren made it a point to talk to Chase as little as possible. Why had she decided, today of all days, she needed to ask him about a birthday party still weeks away?

"I never said your name. No one knows you're here."

"I've got to go." She set her cup down with a *thunk* and rose. Her knee hit the table. Pain shot up her leg. Coffee sloshed onto the oak. "Would you please take me home now?"

"Erika, relax." He smoothed his hands down her arms.

She jerked away.

He raised his hands, as if in surrender, his eyes wary. "Sorry."

She hugged herself. "No, I'm sorry. It's…if she found out…if she knew I was here…"

"She's not going to find out. Why don't you go gather your things? I need to change, and then I'll be ready to go. I already made a list of what we need at the store."

"Okay." She hesitated.

"What?"

"I just thought you were going to take me home first."

"The store is on the way to your house. If you don't mind coming along, it will save some time."

She nibbled on the nail of her ring finger. What if someone saw them together?

"Erika?"

"Um, sure, that's fine." Did anyone the Garretts know live around here? If they did, would they be at the home improvement store this morning? Not likely. Plus, while they were there she could pick up a few more paint swatches. She still hadn't decided on a color

97

for the spare bedroom or the hallway.

"Okay, give me five minutes."

She blew out a breath as he strode from the room. Over the last couple of days, bad luck had followed Erika like a magnet. Should she really be tempting fate further by going to the home improvement store with Chase?

In the living room, she shoved her things into her bag, then folded the blanket and laid it neatly on the couch with the pillow on top. True to his word, in less than five minutes, he sauntered back into the room.

"Okay, I'm set. You ready?" He'd changed into work jeans and a white T-shirt and had his tool belt slung over his shoulder. He slouched against the doorframe. The pose could have been featured in calendars plastered on dorm room walls across the country.

Damn. What was her deal with men in construction gear? Would she react this way to anyone, or did only Chase set her heart tripping? How silly to be worried about being seen with him at the store. If she tore off his shirt and nudged him into the bedroom, no one would see them for days.

She blinked, the sudden mood change making her dizzy. How had she gone from nervous to guilty to aroused in a heartbeat?

Chase.

"Erika?"

"What? Oh. Sorry. Yep, I'm ready."

He'd better fix her plumbing and fast. She really needed a cold shower.

****

At the store Erika stared at the tiny splashes of

color on the paint samples and envisioned what they would look like on her walls. She squinted at them, held them at arm's length, and then brought them closer again. "Arghh."

"What's the matter?" Chase asked.

"How can I make a decision by looking at less than two square inches of a color?"

He laughed. "You could get a few sample bottles and paint a small area on the wall."

She frowned. "Aren't those expensive?"

He shrugged. "Not really. Plus, I can use my contractor's discount for you."

She peered at the colors again. "Well, if you wouldn't mind, that might help."

"Of course not." He went over to the spinning rack holding the sample bottles. "What colors are you—"

"Erika?"

Erika whirled at the sound of her name. She bit back a groan. Louise and Frank's neighbors stood less than two feet away.

"We thought that was you," Evie White said.

"Now isn't this something? We don't usually shop here, but were out this way and came in to pick up a few things. Fancy running into you here," Bob, her husband, added.

Erika gulped. What were the chances? "What a coincidence," she said weakly. Or more bad luck. She made a mental note to never take a trip to Las Vegas. She avoided looking at Chase. Was he far enough away so Evie and Bob wouldn't know they were together?

Nope. Evie's gaze flickered to him. "Well, we didn't mean to interrupt, we just—Aren't you—"

"I'm Sami and Steph's dad," Chase cut in.

"Right. You're Lauren's ex." Based on Evie's tone, she'd not only heard the family's opinion of Chase, but agreed with it as well.

Time to cover her tracks. "Um, I was looking at paint colors for my new place and happened to run into Chase." She waved the samples to give credence to her statement. Would the other woman tell Louise she'd seen them together?

He frowned but didn't contradict her.

"Oh, right. Louise mentioned you'd moved."

Erika nibbled a fingernail. "Yes, I, uh, wanted something without all of the memories. It's been...difficult since Kevin's been...gone." She winced at the nervous chatter. Why was she telling them all this?

Evie patted Erika's arm. "It's always hard to lose someone you love. Especially at such a young age. Kevin was such a good man."

Erika remained silent. What could she say? Behind her, Chase made a sound almost like he was choking. Evie's gaze slid to him. Her eyebrows rose as if wondering why he was still there.

He interpreted the expression correctly. "Well, I should get going. I need to pick up some plumbing supplies for a friend." Was it Erika's imagination he emphasized the last word? He turned to her. "It was nice to see you, Erika. Take care of yourself."

"You, too, Chase." She didn't prolong the eye contact.

"It's such a shame," Evie said when he'd walked away. "Divorce is such an ugly thing. Especially when there's children involved."

Erika couldn't disagree.

Chapter Seven

"Erika?" Chase opened the front door.

"In the closet, down the hall." The muffled words drifted to him.

Puzzled, he followed the sound of her voice. "I'm do—" He stopped. Swallowed. Twice.

Erika stood, partially in the hall closet, her back to him, reaching toward the tall shelf over the bar. With her arms raised, her pink tank top had ridden up revealing a strip of bare skin above the low-riding waistband of her jeans. The jeans stretched tight over the rounded curve of her backside, and the denim hugged her legs all the way down past her ankles. A thin, pink heel peeked out from beneath the hem.

Holy crap.

He cleared his throat, but still the words came out scratchy. "Do you need help with something?"

She turned. "I'm trying to find my 'going out' purse, but I can't see anything at the back of the shelf." She pushed a strand of hair out of her eyes. "It sucks to be short."

He smiled even as his insides tensed. She was going out? Wearing those jeans? He took a step closer. The subtle flowery scent of her perfume wafted to him. He stifled a groan.

"What does it look like?"

"It's small and black with a long strap." Her hands

moved to demonstrate.

He nodded and looked on the shelf. Sure enough, the purse lay against the back wall. He grabbed it, then turned and handed it to her. His gaze swept over her again. Damn she looked amazing. Sexy. "You look nice." What a woeful understatement. "Hot date?" He kept his voice casual, although the thought of her going out with someone caused his stomach to tighten.

He shouldn't be surprised. Erika was young, attractive, and single. Kevin had been gone nearly a year, and hadn't been a good husband in the first place. She needed to move on with her life. Having a date was a good thing. For her.

She looked up at him and grimaced. "Yeah, right. Can you imagine what Mom would say?" she shuddered slightly.

He frowned. "Erika, you can't—"

She held up her hand. "Don't start, okay?"

He sighed. "Okay. So where's 'out' if it's not on a date?" He ignored the relief spreading through him and leaned his shoulder against the doorframe.

"One of the other teachers at school is dating this guy who's a jazz musician. A bunch of us are heading out to hear him play at some bar."

He swallowed the unreasonable panic lodged in his throat. The minute she walked into a bar looking like a teenaged boy's wet dream, she'd have a hundred guys drooling over her. It didn't matter if she didn't have a date this evening. She'd have a dozen offers by the end of the night.

"Sounds like fun." He bit back the irrational impulse to forbid her to go. Who did he think he was?

"Yeah, I guess it will be." Her voice didn't sound

as though she were convinced. "I'm not really into the bar scene, you know?"

"Downtown?"

"Hell no. I definitely wouldn't be going. It's some club out in Evanston."

Well, at least she'd have a rich date. He forced a smile at her words. "I'm sure it'll be fine. Is someone picking you up?"

If his continued line of questioning and rampant curiosity offended her, she didn't show it. She shook her head. "No, I'm driving myself. Which means I can leave whenever I want to." She chewed a hot pink fingernail and looked up at him, a thoughtful expression on her face. Finally she took a deep breath. "Want to come along?"

The invitation surprised him. He hesitated. They'd walked on eggshells around each other since she'd spent the night at his house and they'd run into the Garretts' neighbors at the home improvement store, making polite conversation when necessary, but never discussing anything personal. What had made her drop her guard tonight?

And he hadn't been able to forget their kiss. The memory of her soft lips beneath his kept him awake at night, his body aching and wanting more. Although instinct told him she hadn't asked him out on a date, would spending more time with her, outside of work, simply throw more wood on the fire?

He grimaced at the analogy.

She averted her gaze. "Never mind. I forgot, you, uh, probably have the girls tonight." She turned and walked away from him, but not before he caught the chagrined look on her face.

He cursed, she'd misinterpreted his indecision, and followed her into the kitchen. She was transferring things from a larger purse into the one he'd retrieved from the closet.

"Actually, it's not my night with the girls. I'd like to go with you." After all, someone had to protect her from the legions of adoring males who were likely to descend the minute she walked into the place. It might as well be him. He ignored the niggling thought she might not want protecting. Maybe she wanted to meet someone.

Her gaze met his for one brief instant before sliding away. She still looked slightly embarrassed. "No, that's okay. I don't know why I asked in the first place. I'm sure you have better things to do than hang out with a bunch of teachers listening to Liquid Fire."

"As a mater of fact, I don't have anything to do tonight, and I happen to like jazz music, so I—" He stopped midsentence. "Wait a minute." He raised an eyebrow. "What did you say?"

She giggled, although the sound held a tinge of nervousness. "That's the name of the band."

His eyes widened. "Seriously?"

She nodded, a genuine smile on her lips this time. "Yep. Seriously."

"Oh, man, now I definitely have to come." He smiled at her. "Besides, you already asked. It wouldn't be polite to rescind your invitation." He kept his tone light. Teasing. So she wouldn't know how desperately he wanted to go.

Only to make sure she was all right. If he used the excuse often enough, maybe he'd start to believe himself. But he doubted it.

She rolled her eyes. "Okay, fine, I won't take back my invitation."

"Super." He looked her over, careful not to linger too long on the thrust of her breasts beneath the soft cotton or the curve of her hips. "You look all set. What time are you leaving? Do I have time for a quick shower?"

"Sure. I'm not in any hurry."

"I'll be fast, I promise. I just need to run out to my truck for a change of clothes."

She tilted her head to the side. "Do you always keep extra clothes in your truck?"

He chuckled. "Yeah, I guess I do." He hadn't really thought about it before. He couldn't remember why he'd started the habit, but right now he didn't question it. He winked at her. "Comes in handy for situations like these."

****

Situations like these.

Chase's words stuck in Erika's mind as they made their way into the bar. How often did the situation of going out with a client after work come up?

Of course they weren't going out in the strictest sense of the word. The impulsive invitation to ask him to join her had slipped out before she had time to consider the consequences. She'd alternated between embarrassed, regretful, and glad he'd come along about fifty times since she uttered the words.

Why had she asked him to come?

Because she missed him. Since he'd been working at her house, they'd become reacquainted in a sense. They'd had some really great, meaningful talks. She enjoyed spending time with him. Up until the night she spent at his house and the bad luck of running into Louise and Frank's neighbors the next morning. Since then, the forced politeness had weighed on her.

So she'd invited him along, and now she didn't know how to feel about it. At any rate, too late to change her mind.

She spotted her friends at a table up front near the stage. "There they are," she said over her shoulder.

The warmth of his hand in the small of her back penetrated the thin cotton top as he guided her through the crowd. She swallowed as they drew nearer. Her tummy jumped with nerves. How should she explain Chase to her colleagues?

Before she could worry about it further, Teri looked up and caught her eye. The other woman's gaze slid to Chase and widened, then darted back to Erika's, keen interest visible in it even in the dim light of the bar.

Great. Here we go. Erika took a deep breath. "Hey, sorry I'm late."

Several more pairs of eyes turned at the sound of her voice. Most had a similar reaction to Teri's. At least the women.

"This is Chase," she answered the half a dozen unspoken questions. "My, uh, my brother-in-law."

Teri's mouth formed an O. She held out her hand. "Pleased to meet you, Chase. I'm Teri."

"Likewise." He shook her hand.

After introductions around the table were complete, he procured two chairs from nearby. She slid into the one he held out. He leaned toward her. "I wish you wouldn't call me that."

She ignored the shivery puffs of his breath against

her ear. "Call you what?"

"Your brother-in-law."

She frowned. "What should I call you? My contractor?"

"How about your friend? Or why not simply Chase? Why do we need a label at all?"

"You two want something to drink?" The voice of a server broke into the conversation.

Chase nodded. "I'll have a beer."

"And I'll have a—"

"Long Island iced tea," Chase finished with her.

She laughed and shook her head. "You remember."

"Of course."

Over Chase's shoulder, Erika caught a glimpse of Teri's face. Her eyebrows had once again risen into her hairline. Erika looked away. Boy, was she going to get the third degree later. She couldn't help but glance back at her friend. Teri flashed a thumbs-up.

"Stop it," Erika mouthed.

Chase caught her. He glanced over at Teri, then back at her. "Why don't we change places so you can sit by, Teri, is it?"

"Oh, okay, sure."

They completed the switch and Erika prayed Teri wouldn't say anything with Chase still in such close proximity. But to her credit, Teri was discreet, keeping the conversation general and chit-chatty and including him in it.

"So, how are things coming at your place construction-wise?"

Erika glanced at Chase. "Moving along, wouldn't you say?"

He slid his arm over the back of her chair and

leaned in to include Teri in his response. The woodsy scent of his aftershave tickled Erika's nose. Did he carry that in his truck for *situations like these* as well? "I'd say so. I'm almost finished installing the windows, so I'll start on the porch next."

"Thank God. That thing is a death trap." Teri looked at Erika. "You're lucky no one's fallen through it and sued you."

Chase laughed. "It is in pretty bad shape."

Erika shrugged. "It's an old house. What do you expect? That's why I hired you," she reminded him, a bit more sass in her voice than she'd intended, "to fix some of the things that are in bad shape."

On Chase's other side, Nancy leaned in. "Are you a carpenter?" she asked him.

He turned toward her. "Yes."

"Do you have a card with you? I've been meaning to have a couple of things done around my place."

"Sure." He flexed his hips up to reach for his wallet in his back pocket. Erika's stomach did a tiny flip at the action. She yanked her gaze away. Chase handed Nancy a card. "I specialize in historic rehab and renovation, but I do other work as well."

"Super. I'll be sure to give you a call."

Erika didn't miss the flirty undertones in Nancy's voice. Did Chase hear them as well? Was Nancy someone he'd be interested in? The other woman had joined the faculty only recently and Erika didn't know her very well.

"Great. I'm pretty booked right now, but if you call we can set up an estimate so I can get you on my schedule." Chase slipped into business mode.

"So, you're Erika's brother-in-law?"

Chase darted a look at Erika. She shrugged.

"Are you married to her sister? Or is she married to your brother?" A hopeful note crept into the last question.

"Neither, actually. I used to be married to Erika's husband's sister."

"Used to be?" The hope was more evident now.

"We're divorced."

"Oh, that's too bad." Nancy placed her hand on Chase's arm.

Erika choked on the drink. The alcohol burned down her throat. The stinging pain took her breath away.

Chase turned to her. "Are you okay?" Concern laced his voice.

Erika wiped her watering eyes. "I'm fine," she gasped. "Went down the wrong way."

He nodded and rubbed his hand across her back in a soothing motion. Her insides went quivery.

Teri rejoined the conversation. "Chase, you have two little girls, right?"

"Yeah, Sami and Steph." His tone softened, as it always did, when he spoke of the twins.

"Do you have a picture?"

Once again Chase reached into his back pocket. Erika studiously didn't look, but caught Nancy's gaze focused on his hips. Hussy.

He handed Teri the photograph.

"You're a lucky man."

"I know."

Nancy reached for the picture, leaning into Chase as she did. "Oh, they are adorable." She smiled up at him. "How old are they?"

"They'll be five in a few weeks."

"So they'll be in kindergarten next year. That's what I teach."

"The girls are really excited about it, but I can't believe they're old enough to go to school."

"They do grow up quickly, don't they?"

Before Chase could reply, the lights dimmed further in the bar. The audience hushed as a spotlight lit the stage, highlighting the lone saxophone player off to one side. A bluesy, sensual melody slid over the crowd as he put his fingers to the keys and blew into the mouthpiece.

Chase leaned toward Erika, his arm draped over the back of her chair once again. "He's good." His lips touched her ear as he spoke.

She shivered, but nodded. With him so close, the rest of the room faded as the music wrapped around them. The mellow notes flowed through her, made her bones seem to soften. Liquefy. The heat of Chase's almost touch against her back burned into her.

Liquid. Fire. At the same time. Suddenly the band's name made perfect sense.

Awareness seeped into her. Chase sat close. Her arm touched his chest. His fingers feathered against the bare skin of her shoulder. She breathed in the woodsy, spicy scent of him. More potent now with him so near.

Sexier.

The memory of their kiss filled her mind, her body. Her heartbeat quickened. Her breath became shallow. As if experiencing the feel of his lips against hers again. The taste of him.

She closed her eyes. A mistake. The languid music curled into her soul. It echoed and intensified the feelings inside of her. The awareness became acute. Almost painful.

Beside her, Chase shifted. His thigh brushed hers. She opened her eyes to look at him. He stared down at her. His gaze dropped to her lips. Unconsciously, she slid closer. Raised her face.

Enthusiastic applause broke the spell.

She jumped. Her startled heartbeat matched the tempo of hundreds of clapping hands. She blinked and came back to herself, and after a moment, joined in the applause.

On the pretense of reaching for her drink, she slid her chair away from Chase's. Her hand shook as she took a sip. She willed her pulse to return to normal. Her breathing to become even. For the remainder of the show, Erika kept her distance in the scant inches their separated seats would allow. She recited the Declaration of Independence in her head, trying to block out the sensual pull of the music.

When the lights came up, she exhaled a long breath. The tension ebbed from her tensed muscles.

Chase turned to her, his eyes unfathomable. "Good show."

She nodded. "Yeah, they were really good." She stood. "We, uh, should probably get going."

"Sure." He addressed the rest of the table. "It was nice meeting you all."

"You, too." Teri's gaze found Erika's. "I'll call you tomorrow. So we can chat," she said pointedly.

Erika turned away from the knowing look in her friend's eyes. No doubt about it. She'd be getting the third degree. What had she been thinking, bringing Chase along?

"And I'll give you a call, Chase," Nancy said.

A puzzled frown marred his forehead.

"About the carpentry work?" she prompted.

"Oh, yeah. Right. Sounds good." He nudged Erika with his arm. "You set?"

"Yep. Good night, everyone."

A chorus of good-byes followed as they made their way out of the building. Outside, Erika took a deep breath. The summer humidity had eased with nightfall, and the fresh air filled her lungs and cleared her senses.

They walked without speaking through the parking lot. Her heels clicked on the pavement, accompanied by the heavier tread of Chase's boots. At his truck, he opened the door for her. She scooted in as he walked around to the driver's side.

His door closed with a soft slam, enclosing them in the darkness of the cab. His sexy scent surrounded her in the small space, negating the cleansing effect of the air. He started the engine with a twist of his wrist then reached for the controls of the air conditioner.

"Do you mind if we put the windows down?" she blurted.

He looked at her and raised an eyebrow.

She swallowed. She must have sounded as desperate as she felt. "I-I mean, it's such a pleasant night for a change. It would be nice to have some fresh air."

"Sure. Whatever you want." He pressed a button on his door. Both windows slid down.

She inhaled.

The ride home seemed long. Usually it was easy to talk to Chase. Tonight, now, the words wouldn't come. Her body hummed, hyper-aware of him sitting next to her in the small, confined space. The wind blowing through the windows and tumbling her hair couldn't quite erase the tension.

Finally they reached her house, and he pulled over next to the curb. He turned toward her, but didn't shut off the engine. She held her breath as his gaze roved over her face. It came to rest on her lips.

Would he or wouldn't he? The question had plagued her all night.

"Thanks for inviting me along. I had a good time."

"Yeah, it was nice having someone to drive with." Keep it light. Casual.

A half smile tilted the corner of his mouth. "Right."

She reached for the door handle. "Well, thanks for the ride, then."

"Okay, I'll see you tomorrow."

"Tomorrow?"

He jerked his chin toward the house. "Your windows."

"Oh, right." She blushed and hoped he couldn't tell in the darkened cab.

She opened the door.

"Erika?"

When she turned his face loomed closer than she expected. She forced herself not to pull back. Or lean toward him. "Good night." His lips brushed her cheek.

"Good night, Chase."

****

"You've been holding out on me."

Erika looked up from her desk. After a restless night, she'd decided to get up early and head over to school to work on some units for next year. Leaving the house had accomplished two things. She left before

Chase had arrived, and she put off, at least for a little while, the dreaded phone call from Teri. One she definitely didn't want to have with Chase anywhere near.

Of course, now she needed to face her in person.

In a last ditch attempt to delay the inevitable, she tried for a nonchalant tone. "I don't know what you mean."

"Yeah right." Teri propped a hip on the corner of the desk. "So that's your brother-in-law."

"Yeah, so?"

"Like I said, you've been holding out."

"About?"

Teri snorted. "You know about what. Your brother-in-law," the words sounded sarcastic, "is drop dead gorgeous."

Erika couldn't argue, but didn't want to give Teri a bigger chance to gloat. She shrugged. "I've known him for a long time. He's just Chase."

"Uh-huh, and I'm Wonder Woman."

Erika laughed.

"Seriously, girl, everyone in the bar noticed last night."

"Really, I—"

"Oh, Erika, I'm so glad you're here." Nancy poked her head around the doorframe. "I wanted to ask you something."

"Sure, shoot." Erika waved her in, glad of the reprieve.

The blonde woman walked into the room. She glanced at Teri, as if hoping she'd leave. Teri stared back boldly.

Nancy sighed and turned to Erika. "I, um, I was

wondering about your brother-in-law."

Erika's gaze flicked to Teri, who wore an I-told-you-so expression. "What about him?"

"Well, I wanted to know if he was single. I mean, I know he said he was divorced, but I wondered if he was dating anyone."

Erika went still, but quickly recovered. "I don't think he is. But we don't really talk about things like that."

"Oh. Sure. Sure. But, really, you don't think he is? I mean, he's so hot, how is that possible?" She giggled.

Teri choked off a laugh.

Erika shot her a dirty look then turned back to Nancy. "He's really devoted to his daughters. He spends as much time with them as possible."

Nancy's eyes took on a faraway look. "How sweet." She paused. Bit her lip. "So, do you think he'd go out with me if I asked? He gave me his number. Well, his business number. On his card."

Erika refused to meet Teri's gaze. "I really don't know." Would Chase be interested in Nancy?

"Okay. Well, maybe you can put in a good word for me? You two seem pretty close."

Teri's mouth dropped open.

Erika continued to ignore her. "Sure. I'll see what I can do." When pigs flew.

"Thanks, Erika." She looked at her watch. "Shoot, I need to run. I'll see you ladies later."

"See? What did I tell you?"

"So he's Nancy's type. Maybe she's his. They might be good together." She flipped through a stack of papers on the desk. Her hands shook.

"What?" Teri's outraged gasp echoed in the barren

115

room. "You're not really going to 'put in a good word' for her, are you?"

Erika shrugged. "Why not? Like I said, maybe she's his type."

"She's not."

Erika glanced up, surprised at the finality of Teri's tone. "How do you know?"

"Because I saw the way he looked at you last night. The way he acted around you. And the way you acted around him. You two are totally into each other."

"Don't say that." The words came out sharper than she intended.

"Why not? Maybe it's you two who would be good together."

Erika shook her head. "Yeah. Right. Can you see the looks on Lauren's and Mom's faces if I told them I was dating Chase?" She shivered. "I couldn't do that to them."

"Erika, sweetie, I think it's so great you're still close to Kevin's family. Especially his mom. But you have your own life. Maybe Chase is meant to be a part of it."

"He can't be. I mean, even if I could put aside the whole issue of what my family would think, he doesn't have time for anyone in his life. I wasn't kidding when I said he's devoted to the girls. They mean everything to him. There isn't room in his life for anyone else." A tiny ache stabbed at her heart. "I know what it's like to be second-best. I won't accept that ever again."

"Kevin was a jerk, and we both know it." The words were harsh, but Teri's tone sympathetic. "I agree you deserve better than him. But the way a man feels about his children, and the way he feels about a woman, are two completely different things. I don't think you should discount Chase yet at this point." She rose. "I have to get going, too. Call me if you need to talk." At the door she turned. "And I *definitely* don't think you should ask him about Nancy."

Chapter Eight

"I heard you ran into Chase the other day."

Erika froze. "What?"

"At the home improvement store," Louise said.

Well, that hadn't taken long. Erika had stopped at her mother-in-law's on the way home from school. No sooner had they settled on the patio with tall glasses of lemonade before the topic came up.

Erika took a sip of the iced beverage to sooth her dry throat before answering. "Um, yeah, I was looking at paint colors and, uh, he was there, too."

"That must have been awkward."

Yes, but only because she and Chase had been there together. "He helped me with some color choices."

Louise wrinkled her nose but said, "Well, that was nice of him."

"Yeah, we actually had a nice conversation." Erika pressed her luck to gauge her mother-in-law's reaction.

Louise shook her head. "He seemed like such a nice man at first. I never would have believed he'd give up on his family so easily. To leave those precious girls."

Not exactly the response she'd hoped for. Wouldn't Louise's attitude toward Chase ever soften? "He loves the girls." Erika couldn't help defending him.

The older woman snorted. "He has a funny way of

showing it. What kind of man walks out on his family and only wants to be a part-time father?"

"He sees them every week."

Louise gave her an odd look.

"I mean, isn't that what he and Lauren decided in the custody agreement? He gets them on weekends?" She made it sound like a question.

"It's not the same as always being there."

Ironically, Chase would agree.

"I don't care what's going on in your life," Louise continued. "Nothing is more important than family. And I'll never forgive Chase for tearing this one apart."

****

Chase was packing up when Erika arrived home. The easy, relaxed smile he greeted her with held no trace of the previous evening's sensual tension. "Where have you been all day?"

"School. Then Mom's for a little while."

"School?" His brow furrowed. "Isn't it summer vacation?"

"Yes, but I still have things to work on."

He looked bemused. "I thought that's why teachers were teachers. To get the summer off."

"Well, there is that. But there's a lot more to my career choice than summer vacation," she teased.

He nodded, his tone serious when he replied, "I've seen you with the girls. I bet you're an amazing teacher."

The praise warmed her. "Thanks."

"So, any other crazy teachers working on this beautiful summer day?"

"Funny you should mention that."

He raised an eyebrow.

She stared at the hot pink nail polish on her toe as she traced a wood grain on the floor. "Can I ask you something?"

"Of course."

"Do you ever date?" She wiped sweaty palms on her shorts and hoped she sounded nonchalant. She darted a glance at him. Despite Teri's disapproval, she'd decided to go ahead and ask him about Nancy. Mostly because she wanted to know how he did feel about dating. Not that it mattered for her life. Still, curiosity tugged at her.

For a moment he looked nonplussed. "Sometimes. Why?"

An unexpected stab of jealousy pricked into her. Who did he date? Where did he go to meet women? Where did he take them? "Oh, well, my friend at school asked about you. She seemed, um, interested in you."

Both eyebrows rose. "Interested?"

"Okay, she thought you were really hot."

Chase threw back his head and laughed. "Really?"

"Really." She chewed a fingernail. "Actually, you met her last night. Nancy."

Judging by his vacant expression, the name didn't seem to ring a bell. "Which one was Nancy?"

A secret part of her exalted in the fact he didn't remember. Especially when the other woman had made her interest more than clear. "The one you gave your card to."

His expression cleared. "Oh, yeah, she wanted some work done on her house."

"Chase." Erika shook her head at his naivety. "Do you really think that's why she asked for your card?"

Surprise crossed his face. "Really?" he repeated.

"Really." She studied the floor again. "So, anyway, I'm sure she'd be up for it if you wanted to go out sometime. I mean, I'm not trying to set you guys up or anything, but I know she'll ask me about you again the next time I see her. So if you're interested I can, well, let her know." The words came out in a rush. She glanced up. Then down. "I, um, kind of told her I'd talk to you."

"You did?"

She didn't know how to answer, or even if he expected one, so she remained silent.

"Well, if you see her, tell her I'm flattered, but I don't really have time to date right now. Work keeps me busy in the summer, and I spend whatever free time I have with Sami and Steph."

She nodded and ignored the tiny ache in her heart, even though the words were expected. "Sure, I'll tell her." She risked another glance at him. He looked thoughtful. Almost amused. "What?"

"I'm curious. Can I ask *you* something?"

"O-kay." The word came out hesitant, almost like a question itself.

"What about you?"

"What about me?" She frowned. "I don't think I'm Nancy's type."

His lips quirked. "No, not that. I wondered if *you* thought I was hot."

Erika's brain scrambled. She cast an inadvertent glance down his body. A white T-shirt hugged his chest. The tight sleeves emphasized the toned muscles in his upper arms. His jeans, covered in paint splotches and drywall mud, were worn almost white around the zipper. Her gaze lingered on that very masculine area before she jerked it away. A tool belt hung low around his waist.

She swallowed. Hot might be the understatement of the year.

She opened her mouth. Closed it again. Her gaze met his. The depths danced with amusement. And something else. Something deeper. Darker.

"Never mind. But let me tell you something." He took a step closer. "If I were to go out on a date with someone, it wouldn't be with...what was her name?" He unbuckled the tool belt and let it dangle from his fingertips.

Erika moistened her parched lips with the tip of her tongue. "Nancy," she whispered.

"Whatever." He let the leather strap slide through his fingers until the belt gently touched the floor. He dropped it and took another step. "Do you know who I'd go out with?" He tangled his fingers through the strands of her hair and then raised her face to his.

Her heart thumped erratically. She stopped breathing. He couldn't possibly mean her. Could he?

And then she didn't have to wonder anymore. His mouth covered hers as his hand moved to cup the back of her head. As before, he took complete possession as firm and sure, it worked over hers. His tongue teased her bottom lip. She opened to him and he dipped inside to roll his tongue around hers with slow, languid strokes.

Her knees buckled.

His hands smoothed across her shoulders, down her back, and to her waist. He gathered her close and pulled her against him. She wound her arms around his neck. Pressed closer still.

Without breaking the kiss, he walked her backwards until the back of her knees hit the couch. They gave. Arms securely around her, he eased her down. His weight pressed her into the cushions. Through the denim of his jeans, his arousal thrust against her. Full. Hot. Hard.

He wanted her.

Her heart went wild. Her legs parted to cradle his hips.

His kiss became deeper. More sensual. His tongue darted against hers then withdrew, simulating a more intimate act. Her hands gripped his shoulders. She shuddered. Shivered.

Her pulse pounded in her ears. Blood flowed warm and thick through her veins. An ache began deep inside of her where his hard strength nudged against her. She wanted him, too. She had ever since he'd walked through her door and back into her complicated life.

All the more reason why they needed to stop. On a gasp she tore her mouth from his. His lips moved to her neck. Feathered down to the curve of her shoulder where his teeth bit gently. She jerked against him and almost lost her resolve.

With one last ounce of sanity, she pushed against his chest and tried not to notice how firm the muscles were. "Chase. We can't." The words were breathless. Weak. Unconvincing.

But he heeded them immediately. He levered his body away from hers and shifted them both to a sitting position, although he didn't let her go.

Beneath her ear, his heartbeat thundered. His chest rose and fell in rapid bursts. His harsh breath stirred the wisps of hair loosened from her ponytail. Gradually his breathing slowed.

It took a bit longer, but her pulse eventually returned to a semblance of its pre-kiss pace. Neither made a move to change their position. They sat for long minutes, his arm around her shoulders, her fingers curled in the fabric of his shirt.

Finally he kissed the top of her head. "Are you okay?"

She nodded, although she was far from it, and burrowed deeper into him. His arm tightened.

For a little while longer she let herself enjoy the solid comfort of his embrace. Why did she always associate comfort with Chase's touch? At least when it wasn't generating heart-stopping, knee-weakening, soul-aching pleasure.

Finally she shifted. He let her go. She put some distance between them and smoothed trembling fingers over her hair. Her blood still sang with the memory of his kiss. She blew out a shaky breath. "I-I'm sorry." She couldn't meet his eyes.

"For what?"

"F-for stopping you. I mean, for letting it go so far before I stopped you." She gulped in some air. "We can't do this, Chase."

"I know." The words were soft. Filled with regret. "I should be the one apologizing."

She shook her head.

He ignored her and continued, "I promised you I wouldn't kiss you again. But I'm a weak man. I couldn't resist. You're too damn sexy for your own good." He chuckled. "And mine." He paused. "If things were different…" His voice trailed off.

"But they're not," she said softly. "Everything's

still so"—she groped for the right word—"complicated. Nothing's changed. My family means everything to me. Mom and Dad and…Lauren. I can't lose them. I know you don't understand. And that's okay. You don't have to. But if they ever found out we…we kissed…and we almost…" Her gaze rose to his. "It would devastate them. I can't do this to them. They've been so good to me."

"I do understand. I know how much you love them." He paused. "I wonder if they realize how much you're sacrificing for them." He reached for her hand to trace his fingertip over her knuckles. "Can I ask you something?"

Her pulse accelerated at the light touch. "Yes."

"Are you ever going to move on? It's been a year since Kevin died. Don't you want to get married again?"

She shrugged. "Maybe someday."

"You deserve to find someone who will treat you the way a real man should. Cherish you. Love you. Someone who will get down on his knees everyday and thank God for you."

Moisture welled in her eyes. For a moment she wanted desperately for Chase to be the man he described. The one who would cherish her. Love her. But he couldn't be the one. "Maybe it's not meant to be for me." Her voice shook with unshed tears.

"I don't believe that."

A tear spilled over and trickled down her cheek. He cupped her face and wiped the moisture away with his thumb. "Please don't cry. I didn't mean to make you sad." He drew her back into his arms.

"I know," she mumbled against his chest.

"I wish I could be that man."

Her heart stuttered. Stopped. Started again.

"I have nothing to offer you. Even if you were ready to move on." He shook his head. "I don't ever want to get married again."

She squeezed her eyes shut. The words caused an ache in her chest, even though they didn't surprise her.

"You deserve someone who will give you everything you've ever wanted." He sighed. "I never wanted marriage. A family. I wound up with it all. The marriage part didn't turn out so great for me, but I'll always be grateful to Lauren for one thing. She gave me my girls. I can't imagine not having Sami and Steph in my life. I love them more than I thought it was possible to love another person." He hesitated. "I'm not sure there's room in my heart for anyone else."

Erika swallowed back the hurt. She appreciated his honesty. At any rate, a future with Chase was impossible. For a multitude of reasons. The ones they'd recently covered for starters.

But his kisses had awakened something inside of her. Something she hadn't realized she'd been missing. And now she yearned for it. For a man in her life. A man who would treat her how Chase described. Want her. Cherish her. Love her. Make her the most important thing in his life.

Even if she could somehow get past how her family would react, he couldn't be that man. She'd never let herself settle for being second to anyone ever again. Not even his children.

So why did she desperately want him to be the one?

"Can I ask you something else?"

She straightened out of his arms. She couldn't think clearly with him touching her. "Sure." She folded her legs beneath her on the couch.

"Why did you ask me to come to the bar with you last night?"

She smiled in chagrin. "I've been asking myself the same thing." How could she answer without giving too much away? "I'm not sure. It was an impulse."

"I mean, don't get me wrong. I'm glad you did, but I know you're afraid someone will see us together. Again. You're scared the family will find out I'm working here, and then out of the blue, you ask me to go out with you...well, not out, but you know what I mean."

"Yeah, I guess I do seem kind of flighty." Problem was, when her heart, not to mention her suddenly raging hormones, got involved, all her common sense flew out the window.

He shook his head. "No, you don't. I'm just curious. What made you change your mind last night?"

She looked at him, and then went for broke and laid it on the line. "I missed you. I hate how...polite we've been to each other since I spent the night at your house. I wanted to get things back to the way they were when you first started working here. I want to be able to talk to you. I know it's selfish. I can't have it both ways. You. My family.

"But I lose my head when you're around. I can't think straight." Heat crept into her cheeks. "Sometimes I lose all sense of what's right and wrong when I look at you." A nervous laugh escaped. "You *are* hot." She rushed on before he could comment. "But more than anything, you're you. I can talk to you. And when we're together, it doesn't feel wrong. It's comfortable and familiar…and right. I forget all the reasons it's wrong."

Silence fell. Her words hung in the stillness.

"I'm sorry," she said at last. "You've been so understanding about my family and how I feel about them. And you've been honest with me about where you stand." She glanced up at him. "I thought I should be honest with you."

He nodded. A bemused smile curved his lips. "I'm glad you were." He hesitated. "Well, I guess we've gone through all the reasons why we can't be together, so there's only one thing I need to know." He paused and looked into her eyes. "Will you go out with me Friday night?"

Chapter Nine

Going out with Erika might be the most irrational decision Chase had ever made. Which said a lot. After all, he'd made a lot of not so bright choices in his life. This one might top them all.

In a bizarre, fantastic, wonderful way.

What had gotten into him? He'd asked her out on a date. A real, live, bona fide date. After all they'd talked about, he went and did it anyway.

He couldn't offer her what she deserved. A future with a decent guy. A guy who would marry her and cherish her and give her everything she'd always wanted. That guy couldn't be him. Because he had no intention of ever getting married again. Hell, he'd never intended to in the first place. In his mind, marriage didn't come close to the happily ever after promised in fairy tales.

Proof abounded, not even counting his own disastrous experience. His parents' marriage had been, and still was, miserable. His sister was divorced. Many of his friends were already divorced. Marriage as an institution, let alone a life-long commitment, wasn't feasible, or even logical.

He'd planned on avoiding it at all costs. But then Lauren had gotten pregnant. He'd wanted to be the decent guy there. Take responsibility. Do the right thing. Look where it had gotten him. Divorced, with his two precious daughters caught in the middle of their parents' bitterness.

He wouldn't go down that road again. He had nothing to offer Erika. Nothing at all. But it didn't stop him from being selfish enough to want her.

Chase had been honest with her, though, as she'd been honest with him. Told her how he felt. Where he stood. He didn't want to mislead her. Promise her something he couldn't give.

To say he'd been stunned when she accepted his date would be putting it mildly. But she had. Knowing what she did. Knowing he had nothing to offer.

Part of him wanted to know why she'd said *yes*. Especially since she had plenty of her own reasons to say no. But the rest of him didn't want to ask. Because he feared she'd change her mind. And outside of spending time with Sami and Steph, nothing in a long while had made him happier than anticipating the coming night.

****

Erika took a critical look at herself in the full-length mirror. Behind her, a mountain of discarded clothing covered the bed. The black dress she'd finally decided on had a fitted bodice held up by thin spaghetti straps. The soft fabric flared over her hips, ending in a full skirt right above her knees. Strappy sandals with three-inch heels made her legs look long and sleek.

She twisted to peer over her shoulder. She'd straightened most of the curl from her hair, leaving soft waves to brush the bare skin of her back. Facing forward again, she rechecked her makeup for the thousandth time. Her hand shook as she applied a layer of gloss over her lipstick. It had been a long time since she'd been out on a date. She really shouldn't be going on one with Chase.

But the excited hum coursing through her outweighed the queasy tingle of misgiving in her stomach. Since he'd asked, she'd thought of little else. Even the fear of her family finding out hadn't been enough to dull the keen anticipation.

The doorbell rang. Her gaze flew once more to her reflection. Framed by lashes darkened with mascara and liner, her eyes sparkled with expectancy. Her hands trembled as they smoothed over her skirt. With a final fortifying breath, she headed down the stairs.

Willing her pulse to slow, she opened the door. The breath promptly whooshed out of her lungs when Chase smiled down at her. She allowed her gaze to drift from the compelling depths of his for a moment. He wore a light gray shirt. A tie, in a slightly darker shade, was knotted around his neck. Black slacks encased his legs. The semi-formal attire made him look dashing and debonair. And sexy. In a completely different way than his work clothes did.

Her glance returned to his. His eyes glittered with the same suppressed excitement hers had in the mirror. He held out a calla lily.

"You remembered." Her voice shook. The flower had always been her favorite.

"Yes." He leaned down to brush a kiss across her cheek. The scent of his aftershave tickled her nose. She closed her eyes and inhaled.

"Are you set? We have a bit of a drive ahead of us. I figured you'd be more relaxed if I chose a restaurant not so close to home."

His thoughtfulness moved her. "I'm ready." She

held up the lily. "But let me put this in water before we go. I'll only be a minute."

He followed her to the kitchen. When she turned from the cabinets, she started to find him standing so close. The intent in his eyes made her heart skip a beat. He took the bloom from her suddenly lifeless fingers and set it on the counter behind her. His arm wrapped around her waist and drew her close. "If we don't get this out of the way now, neither of us is going to be able to think about anything else." His minty breath feathered her face as his head lowered. "It's not often I get to take a beautiful woman out to dinner. And I, for one, would like to enjoy every aspect of the evening." The words whispered against her lips before his mouth covered hers.

She opened to his kiss and pressed even closer to him. Her hand rose to the back of his neck where her fingers threaded through his hair. The other hand rested on his chest. Beneath the silky cotton, his heartbeat raced beneath her palm.

His lips, warm, wet, and sure, moved with hers. Her head spun as the kiss deepened. Their moist breath mingled. Her pulse sprinted to catch up with his. When he pulled away, she tightened her fingers in his hair to prolong the kiss. Her heart exalted as he gave in. His mouth pressed more urgently over hers.

After several long, delicious moments, he gentled the pressure. This time she let him go, but bit back a whimper when his lips left hers.

She opened her eyes to gaze up at him. His irises looked like pools of melted chocolate. The soft pink of her lipstick tinted his mouth. With her index finger, she wiped it away. "We both don't need to wear lipstick to dinner." She tried for a teasing tone, but the words trembled. As did her limbs.

His lips quirked. "Probably not." His voice came out huskier than usual.

She turned her attention to the lily on the counter and willed her nerves into some semblance of order. "Okay, now I'm set," she said after placing the delicate bloom in a vase.

Outside, he held the door of his truck open so she could climb up onto the seat. She reached into her purse for her lipstick to reapply it.

"I'm just going to kiss if off again later," Chase said.

Her breath caught at the provocative threat.

At the restaurant, after they'd given their orders to the waiter, he studied her across the white cloth covered table. His dark eyes reflected the small candle that flickered between them. He raised his wineglass in a toast. "Here's to breaking all the rules."

She clinked her glass against his before sipping the wine. Its light, fruity flavor teased her tongue.

"So, why did you decide to break the rules and come out with me tonight?" His throaty chuckle made her tummy flip-flop. "Don't get me wrong, I'm not complaining."

She shrugged, unsure how to answer. She'd second-guessed her motives and her agreement since the moment he asked her. Finally she decided on the truth. "Because I wanted to." She didn't have any better excuse for her behavior. And damn if she could make herself regret it.

His eyes darkened, but then he looked away. "Are we crazy? Doing this?"

Her heart squeezed at the thought of him having regrets, but she answered with a smile. "Probably." She twirled the wineglass, studying the pearly liquid as it clung to the side of the glass. "Why did you ask me?"

He grinned. "Because I wanted to."

****

Chase pulled to the curb in front of Erika's house and cut the truck's engine. For a moment they sat in the silence. He turned toward her and laid his arm across the back of the seat. The moonlight shining through the windshield revealed a play of emotion in his eyes she couldn't quite interpret.

"Thanks for coming to dinner with me." His soft words surrounded her in the confining space.

"You're welcome."

"I had a good time."

"Me, too." Erika found she couldn't utter more than those simple, oft-used syllables. It had been so long since she'd been on a date, she wasn't sure what came next. Should she invite him inside? Was he expecting something from her? Where did they go from here?

The hand behind her moved. His fingers slid up into her hair. She turned to him. The expression in his eyes changed, the irises darkening to a deep mocha. His hand cupped the side of her face, and his thumb traced over her cheek with feather-light strokes.

She shivered as his gaze caressed her features with the same soft intensity. The woodsy scent of his cologne washed over her as he leaned closer, drew her face upward, and lowered his lips. As the firm pressure of his mouth closed over hers, she sighed in contentment. His mouth worked against hers with

134

gentle persuasion, enticing her to open to him. When she did, he slipped his tongue into the warm recess of her mouth, where it mated with hers in a sensual dance. He tasted like wine and heat and sin.

Tiny shivers of desire sped along her nerves, and Erika shuddered when Chase pulled his lips from hers to trail a hot, moist path down the column of her throat. She arched her neck. He bestowed nibbling bites to the tender flesh on his way back up to her mouth. A growl vibrated through him as he held her against the solid wall of his muscled chest. His mouth consumed hers once again.

The kiss became more urgent. With his arms banded around her and not even a whisper's breath between them, each shuddering breath he took echoed her wildly beating heart. Just when she thought she couldn't take any more, he gentled the kiss, withdrawing his tongue and sipping softly at her lips, before breaking the contact altogether. He rested his forehead against hers while he struggled to catch his breath.

Erika fought the same battle. A pulse pounded in her ears and echoed back to her in the cab of the truck. Finally he pulled a deep gulp of air into his lungs and moved away from her. His gaze searched hers for a moment before he spoke. "I'll walk you to the door."

Exiting the truck, he walked around the hood to open the door. He clasped her elbow in a gentle grip and helped her step down. Her shaking legs hit the pavement, and it took a second to steady herself. His grasp tightened. Would he kiss her again at the door? Would he ask to come in? Would she be able to stop herself from inviting him in if he didn't?

But at the door he paused and shoved his hands in the pockets of his pants. He waited while she retrieved the keys from her purse. Once her trembling fingers got the lock undone, she turned to him, but once again found she didn't know what to say.

"I'll see you on Monday." Chase's voice broke the intense silence.

"Monday?"

"It's the weekend and I have the girls, so I can't see you before then. But I'll be here bright and early Monday morning for work."

She nodded.

He lifted a hand as if to touch her face, but instead dropped it and shoved it back into his pocket. "Good night," he whispered.

"Good night." He made it halfway down the sidewalk before she called to him. "Chase?" He turned. "Why didn't you ask to come in?" The words were out before she could stop them.

Chase went very still and considered her for a moment. She nibbled her fingernail. Why had she asked? Would he ask now, since she'd been the one to bring it up? Did she want him to ask?

After a long, heart-stopping moment, he spoke. "I don't want you to think that's all I want from you." He turned and walked to his truck. The engine roared to life, and then he pulled away from the curb.

Erika let herself into the house then leaned against the door. The after-effects of his kiss ran through her. She raised a shaking hand to push the hair away from her face. Her legs trembled. Blood flowed thick and hot in her veins. Her pulse pounded.

His words left her with more questions than

answers. She couldn't have a long-term relationship with him. He didn't want a permanent relationship with her. She accepted his reasons, and he hers, but she'd also accepted his date. So if he didn't want to sleep with her, what else could he possibly want?

****

Chase sat and stared at the empty fireplace in the living room. He loosened his tie with one hand, and then raised the tumbler he held in the other to his lips. The fiery whiskey burned down his throat as he tossed it back. The heat settled in his stomach, but didn't come close to matching the fire consuming the rest of his body.

He ached. For Erika.

He wanted her. So why hadn't he asked to spend the night? Judging by her response to his kisses, and her question at the door, she probably would have said yes. Right now they could be naked, tangled in the sheets of her bed, learning each other's secrets.

The ache became a throb. He splashed more whiskey into the glass and gulped it down.

What did it say about him if he would have asked? His response to her question taunted him. Mostly because he didn't know the answer to it himself. What did he want from her, besides the obvious?

He definitely didn't want to be the guy who took a woman out and expected sex at the end of the date. He hadn't expected sex, but he'd be honest and admit he wanted it. Wanted Erika. But he had nothing more to offer, and he wouldn't treat her so callously. She deserved better.

With a sigh, he rose from the chair, recapped the bottle before putting it away in the cabinet above the fridge. He twisted the key in the lock to secure the doors.

In the bathroom, he stripped off his clothes, leaving them in a careless pile on the floor. He reached into the shower and turned the knob. Water cascaded into the tub. He adjusted the temperature until the icy cold water numbed his fingers, and then stepped under the spray.

****

"I kissed Chase."

Teri's mouth dropped open in comical fashion. The cup of iced coffee in her hand froze halfway to her lips. "What?" She blinked. "When? Where?" She shook her head as if in a daze and narrowed her eyes. "Spill, girl."

Erika chewed her fingernail and avoided Teri's gaze. "In the kitchen. The first time."

Teri's eyes popped wider. She lowered her drink without taking a sip. "The first time? You kissed him more than once?"

Erika nodded. "I…uh, I think we're dating. Sort of."

"You think you're dating sort of." Teri made circles with her hand. "Okay, start at the beginning." She leaned forward and placed her elbows on the table.

"Well, you know when Nancy asked me to see if Chase was interested in her?"

Teri frowned. "Oh, I remember. And you were actually going to ask him."

"Well, I did. I told him about Nancy and—"

"You did what?" Indignation colored Teri's outburst.

"Are you going to let me finish?"

Teri made a locking motion over her lips.

"Thank you. Anyway, after I asked him about

138

Nancy, he said he wasn't interested in her. He wasn't interested in dating at all. But then he kissed me again. Later we talked about why it wasn't a good idea for us to go out." She took a deep breath. "But then he asked me on a date for last night. So we went to dinner."

Teri's mouth opened and closed, but no words came out.

Erika could almost see the wheels turning in Teri's mind. She didn't know if she expected a reprimand in the form of 'Are you crazy?' or approval in the form of a 'You go, girl.' from her friend. Finally, she couldn't stand the suspense any longer. "Say something, please," she pleaded.

"Is he a good kisser?"

Erika's face flamed. "That's not exactly what I meant." She lowered her gaze to the uneaten muffin in front of her. She picked at it with a purple fingernail. "Yes. Like weak-in-the-knees, turn me inside-out good."

Teri collapsed back against her chair. "Wow," she breathed.

"That, too."

"Right." Teri fell silent for a moment, but her face held a question.

"What?"

"So…" Teri let the word trail off.

"So?" Erika prompted.

"So, boxers or briefs?"

Erika shook her head in amusement. "I don't know."

Teri studied her, a shrewd look on her face. "But you want to find out, don't you?"

Heat suffused Erika's cheeks again, and she looked

down at the crumbled remains of the muffin. "Yes." She'd never been able to lie convincingly to Teri, why bother trying to start now?

"Oh boy."

Erika raised her gaze. "Oh boy is right. What am I going to do?"

Teri smiled. "I think the answer is pretty obvious."

"Is it?" Erika only wished it could be as simple as it sounded.

"Come on, go for it. I don't think there's anything wrong with you hooking up with Chase. Indulge yourself.

You deserve a little happiness in your life. It's okay, you know."

"I know. It's just…"

"What?"

"It would be so…so selfish to get involved with Chase."

"So what? It's okay to be selfish every once in a while."

Erika shook her head. "Once in a while? Everything I do is selfish."

Teri raised an eyebrow. "What do you mean? You're one of the most unselfish people I know."

Erika lowered her eyes. "That's not true." She studied the empty cup in front of her. The ice shifted as it melted. "Why do you think I never told them Kevin was cheating on me?"

Teri grimaced. "You didn't want to hurt them. See? Unselfish. Personally I think they need to know what a slimy, cheating bastard he was," she muttered.

Erika ignored the last comment. "Not hurting them was part of it, but only a little part." Her gaze met

Teri's again then flicked away. "Mostly I didn't tell them because I was afraid of losing them."

"How would you lose them if they found out about Kevin?"

"Well, if they knew he didn't love me anymore, maybe they wouldn't either."

"Girlfriend, that doesn't make one lick of sense. Especially since he's"—she hesitated—"gone. Don't you think they should know?"

Erika shook her head vehemently. "No. Why add to their hurt?" She'd said similar words to Chase weeks ago. Back when things had been only a little complicated. Now they were a lot complicated. "Besides, telling them about Kevin wouldn't make any difference in how they feel about Chase."

"No, I guess you're right about that."

"So, back to the original question. What are you going to do?"

Erika sighed. "Damned if I know."

****

The question continued to taunt her as she lay in bed trying to sleep.

Getting involved—more involved—with Chase was stupid. Asinine. Insane. Dangerous. So why even consider it? Why not end things now? Walk away before anyone got hurt.

The ache in her heart gave her part of her answer. Walking away from Chase would hurt. Shouldn't she have at least one really great memory to counteract the pain? They'd already crossed a line with their relationship. Why not go one step further? Why not go where they both obviously wanted to go?

Why did it have to be so difficult? Why analyze it

to death and make it even more complicated? Neither of them wanted a long-term relationship. So why not indulge in a little pleasure? Why not find out if he did prefer boxers or briefs? Why not find out if he was as good in real life as he was in her dreams?

The questions plagued her throughout the night. By three in the morning she'd tossed and turned so much the bed looked like a war zone. She kicked her way out of the tangled mess of covers. Without turning on the lamp, she made her way down to the kitchen. She yanked open the freezer and blinked in the harsh glare of its light. Ignoring the carton of low-fat vanilla, she retrieved the double chocolate chunk. Not bothering with a bowl, she sat at the table then dipped a spoon into the decadent treat. The rich, creamy ice cream slid down her throat. A blissful sigh whispered through her lips.

In the dark, the house creaked and settled around her in the comforting way only old buildings can do. Soon the spoonfuls of chocolatey goodness she consumed at a steady rate helped her to relax. The tension left her shoulders. The knot of unease loosened in her stomach.

By the time Erika's spoon scraped the bottom of the carton, a peaceful lassitude flowed through her. She tossed the empty container in the recycling bin, gave the spoon one final lick before setting it in the sink, and headed back upstairs.

Chapter Ten

The next morning, the peaceful feeling remained. Indulging in the decadent early morning therapy session had freed her to think about indulging in other sinful things as well. To be specific, indulging in Chase.

Such indulgences didn't last. Eventually the desserts ran out. The important thing was to savor those last blissful moments. Grab a spoon or a fork and enjoy it while it lasted. The last scoop of ice cream. That last bite of creamy cheesecake. Chase.

Erika swung her legs over the side of the bed. "Okay, Chase, get ready to be forked." She giggled a little at her dirty play on words as she headed for the shower.

She shaved her legs, even above the knees, twice. Today was the day. If Chase still hadn't figured out what he wanted from her, well, she'd let him know. She wanted to do something reckless.

She'd always been the one to lay low. Avoid conflict. Not cause any waves. Any trouble. She was always the good girl.

For once she wanted to do something irresponsible. She wanted to be bad. Because in this case, it would be so good. She wanted to do Chase. Damn the consequences.

So what if he couldn't offer her a long-term relationship? So what if he had no room in his heart for her? At the moment her interest lay in a region decidedly south of his heart.

An image of soft, worn denim outlining the masculine area popped into her head. Her reflection in the mirror wavered as her eyes glazed over. She licked her lips as anticipation coursed through her at the thought of taking their relationship to the next level.

She'd even come up with a label. A summer fling. Also known as sex, no strings attached. It had been a long time since she'd been flung.

She snorted. Hell, who was she kidding? She'd never been flung. Play by the rules was her motto. Play it safe. She always had. Until now. She'd broken a lot of rules with Chase lately. The time had come to break the biggest one of all. They needed to get flinging before summer drew to a close.

Erika's nerves buzzed eagerly when Chase walked into her house fifteen minutes later. "Hi." He greeted her with a kiss.

The tension notched higher.

He held up two paper cups. "I brought coffee."

"No coffee this morning."

"Wha—?" Chase stopped when she took the containers from him.

She set them on the table in the entryway, grabbed his hand, and pulled him toward the stairs. He followed her up, a puzzled frown on his face. She led him into the master bedroom then stopped next to the bed. He glanced down at it before his gaze met hers. Something deep and dark flickered in his eyes. Good. It wouldn't take him long to catch on. Her tummy tightened.

"Erika, what—"

"I'm through waiting."

His gaze darted to the bed and back to her again. The flicker in his eyes deepened, as did his tone. "For what?"

"You." She stripped her T-shirt over her head and dropped it to the floor.

His gaze slid down her body. It paused at her lacy bra before traveling back up to hers. The ember in his eyes blazed to life. He swallowed. "I…you…we…"

"Exactly." She took a step closer and splayed her hand over the fabric covering his chest. It rose and fell with the disjointed rhythm of his uneven breath. Beneath her palm, his heart raced.

"Chase, I know what I'm doing," she answered the unspoken question in his eyes. An unquenched fire, tempered with indecision, burned in their dark depths. "I understand how you feel about relationships and marriage. I'm not expecting anything from you. Even if you felt differently, *I* couldn't accept anything more.

"This is all I want. Here. Now. You." Her hand slid down to his stomach. The muscles tensed. She slipped beneath the hem of his T-shirt to touch his bare flesh.

His breath caught. Held.

"I want you." She skimmed his shirt up, exposing the flat plain of his stomach. Her breath halted when she uncovered the firm, sculpted muscles of his chest, covered with a light dusting of hair. He offered no resistance, but raised his arms so she could tug the T-shirt over his head.

When he lowered them, his hands came to rest at her waist. The skin on his palms was slightly rough on her bare flesh. He pulled her toward him until their hips met. His arousal thrust against her. The breath she'd been holding whooshed out in a shuddery sigh. Yep, he'd definitely caught on. Anticipation curled through her.

Trapped between their bodies, her arms pressed into the unyielding wall of his chest. Her hands rested on his shoulders. She ran her fingers over the ridge of his collarbone. One of his hands slid up her back. He brushed her hair away to expose her neck. His thumb feathered over the pulse jumping in her throat. He hooked a finger beneath the strap of her bra and drew it down one shoulder.

All the while he watched her. The fire in his eyes grew hotter, smoking and sparking, until it threatened to consume her with its heat. She pulled out of his arms. He let her go. She took his hand as she lay back on the bed. He followed her down, lying beside her and propping his head on one hand.

With the other he traced circles on her abdomen. She shivered under his light caress. The hungry look in his eyes touched her soul. Nothing could be more perfect than this moment. With slow deliberation, he untied the string at the top of her shorts. She raised her hips so he could slide them down her legs. He dipped his head to kiss her navel. She squirmed beneath his ministrations when his tongue dipped into the indentation.

The shivery tingle spread. Heat followed in its wake when his mouth moved to her breast. Through the lace of her bra, he sucked the nipple. The damp fabric rubbed against the sensitive tip as his tongue stroked over her.

Her vivid dreams paled in comparison to the reality of his touch on her. "Better than my dreams," she murmured.

He lifted his mouth from her breast and raised his eyes, filled with burning wonder, to hers. "Your dreams? You dream about me?" His thumb brushed the tightened nipple. "Like this?"

Her back arched. "Yes," she managed even as a bolt of white-hot desire zigzagged from the sensitive tip of her breast straight to her womb.

"Tell me about them." The command was soft. Sexy. Intimate.

She shook her head with a teasing smile. Her hand feathered down his chest and past his navel, to cup him through the denim of his jeans. His hips bucked as his breath hissed out.

"Haven't you ever heard that actions speak louder than words?" With deliberate care, she eased the zipper down then slid her hand into the widened V. "Mmmn. Boxers."

"Is that a good thing?" His voice shook.

"Mmm hmmmnnn. Very sexy."

"Oh yeah?"

"Yeah." Beneath her exploring fingers he grew harder. Hotter. She kissed the pulse at the base of his neck. "Take your jeans off," she whispered.

"Your wish is my command." He shoved the jeans down his legs. "Do I do that in your dreams?" he murmured. His palm grazed the skin on the back of her knee. "Or this?" He hitched her leg over his hip.

Her head fell back. Heat spread through her until her limbs grew heavy. "Definitely."

His lips found the soft underside of her jaw. She shivered. They rolled until she lay on her back with him above. He splayed his hand on her chest, stroking down between her breasts, over her stomach, until he caught the elastic of her panties with his finger. He slid them down her legs.

He shifted to take off his boxers. She stilled his hand with her own. "No, don't."

He raised an eyebrow.

"Leave them on," she whispered. She reached into the slit at the front and drew him out.

"Another dream?" His voice caught as she explored him with gentle fingers.

She shrugged. "Maybe," she teased.

"Creative." The word sounded as though it took an effort to say.

"I don't...I didn't think about..." She bit her lip. "Do you have...protection?"

He nodded. "In my wallet." He pulled away to grab his jeans from the floor. Before she could miss the heat of his body too much, he was back. "Now, where were we?"

"Right here." She wrapped her arms around his neck and tugged him down for a kiss. The sweet heat of his mouth made her head spin. When the tip of his tongue touched hers, tiny pulses of electricity zipped through her to settle between her thighs, where the hot length of him pressed against her.

He shifted, pulling away a slight bit before thrusting forward and into her. She hooked her leg around the back of his knee, drawing him further into her warmth. He remained still for a moment. She savored the feel of him pulsing full and hard inside of her. She raised her hips. He sank deeper.

She shuddered as flames licked through her veins, singeing her from the inside out. He moved, gliding against her slick walls. Again and again and again. The fire blazed hotter, brighter, lighting up the darkened space behind her closed lids. With a blinding burst, she combusted. Her body exploded around him, as with a final thrust, he joined the conflagration. The scorching inferno raged for endless moments before consuming itself.

Her blood still simmering, Erika panted. Above her, his chest rose and fell in a rapid cadence. His harsh breath stirred the damp strands of hair and tickled her neck.

After a minute he rolled away, but soon turned back to gather her into his arms. She cuddled against him. The accelerated beat of his heart raced beneath her ear.

After a while he spoke. "Wow." The word vibrated against her cheek.

She laughed and kissed his chest. "Not a bad way to start the day, huh?"

"Best breakfast I've had in a long time."

She propped herself on an elbow to look down at him. "Sorry you didn't get your coffee." She kept the conversation light, hoping he wouldn't hear the betraying emotion in her voice. She'd known sex with Chase would be fabulous. What she hadn't known was how earth-shattering the experience would be. Her whole world had tilted, re-centering itself around him.

He rolled his eyes. "Yeah, 'cause that's what I'm thinking about right now."

She traced a path through the soft whorl of hair on his chest with her finger. "So, can I talk you into taking the day off?" Once had definitely not been enough to satisfy her craving. Would it ever be satisfied? The notion it might not scared the beejeezus out of her.

He chuckled. "Well, considering you're the boss, I'm sure we can come to some kind of agreement." He skimmed his finger over the strap of her bra then slid beneath it to trace the delicate ridge of her shoulder. "What did you have in mind instead?" The husky note of his voice told her he could guess the answer.

She leaned down to kiss his neck. Her lips slid up to his ear. "What would you say to not leaving this bed all day long?" She nipped the lobe.

"I'd say I like the way you think." In a move so sudden she didn't see it coming, he flipped her over so their positions were reversed. "Second course, coming up," he murmured before his lips claimed hers.

****

True to their word, they spent most of the day in bed, leaving only to take care of the most basic fundamentals. Now, night blanketed the room as she once again lay in his arms.

"You still awake?" The soft words reached her in the velvet darkness.

"I can't sleep."

He hesitated before answering. "You're used to being alone here."

"No, it's not that. I mean, yes, I'm used to being alone..." Her voice trailed off.

"But?"

"I don't want to fall asleep."

"Why?" Puzzlement laced his voice.

"I don't want to miss any of this. The feel of your arms around me. The beat of your heart. The brush of your fingers across my skin." She trailed her fingers over his chest. The darkness made her brave. Able to speak her mind. "I'm afraid I'll wake up, and you'll be

150

gone. Maybe this is all one of my wonderful dreams."

The hand at her back stilled. "You're not dreaming." He paused. "You really do dream about me?"

"Yes."

"Since I kissed you?"

She hesitated. Should she tell him?

The warmth of his skin next to hers decided her. They'd shared themselves with each other today, making it easy to believe they had no secrets from one another. She had so many secrets in her life. She didn't want to keep this one from him. "For a long time now."

"How long?"

"Since that night I fell asleep in your arms last year."

He went still. Even his breath ceased.

Had she admitted too much? What would he think of her?

"Will you tell me about them now?" he asked after a moment. He'd made similar requests throughout the day, but she teasingly declined, showing him instead of telling.

She burrowed into him. "A lot came true today."

"A lot? Not all of them?"

Her face flamed. She was glad the shadows hid her. "No, not all."

Silence fell. Her words hung in the darkness. "Well," he said finally. "We'll have to see about acting out the rest."

Her heart sped at the provocative promise.

"But for now, I want you to go to sleep. I promise, you're not dreaming right now."

She couldn't agree. How could lying there with

Chase be anything but a dream?

As always, he read her mind. "Should I pinch you to prove you're not dreaming?" His soft laugh rumbled beneath her ear.

She smiled. "No."

"Well, then, I'll tell you what. If I promise to be here in the morning, will you go to sleep?" His arm tightened around her, as if to underscore his words.

She snuggled closer to him. "That sounds like something you'd say to the girls."

"Well, see, then you know it's true. I'd never break a promise to them." He kissed the top of her head. "Now, go to sleep. I'll see you in the morning."

Even with his assurance, Erika didn't drift off right away. She hadn't been honest with Chase earlier. Not completely. Most of what she'd told him had been true. About wanting him. Then. Now. But she'd discovered something during the course of the day. The wonderful, magical, better than any dream she ever had day they spent in her bed. She wanted him for a lot longer than right now. Maybe for the rest of her life.

Of course that couldn't happen. So, like so many other things in her life, her love for Chase would never be anything more than another secret to keep.

****

Long after Erika had fallen asleep, Chase lay awake staring at the shadowed ceiling. He wouldn't break his promise. He'd be there in the morning. Of course he would.

Breaking that particular promise to Erika didn't worry him. What worried him was he wanted to promise her more. He wanted to promise her forever, but the concept had no meaning. Forever had been part of his wedding vows. Look where it had gotten him. Erika and Kevin had vowed to love each other forever. He'd cheated on her right up until his death.

Forever was a meaningless word. Forever hadn't worked out for him and Lauren. And it certainly hadn't worked out for Erika and Kevin. Or her father and his many wives. Or Chase's parents. How could he even be thinking of applying the word to himself and Erika? Hadn't experience taught him anything at all?

So where did they go from here? Erika deserved forever. And he couldn't be the guy to give it to her.

Chapter Eleven

"What did you decide to do about Chase?" Teri asked.

Erika's cheeks flamed and she looked down at her lunch as erotic memories washed through her. She snagged a fry, chewed, and swallowed before answering. "I decided to fork him."

Teri's eyes popped wide. Her hands froze with her burger halfway to her mouth. "Excuse me?"

Erika laughed. "Pun intended. I decided to enjoy him while he lasts."

Teri arched a brow. "While he lasts?"

Erika shrugged. "It's a summer fling, remember? Summer won't last forever."

Teri finally took a bite of her burger. She contemplated Erika while she chewed. "Are you sure that's all it is?" she asked after swallowing.

Erika avoided Teri's perceptive gaze. "Of course that's all it is." She fiddled with another fry. "There can't be anything else."

"Are you sure?"

Erika glanced up. "I'm sure." She offered a wry smile. "We've had this conversation before, remember?"

"Oh, I remember." Teri paused as if weighing her next words. "I wondered if you'd changed your mind...since everything became a little more than hypothetical."

Erika shook her head. "No," she said quietly. "I haven't changed my mind. Nothing has changed."

"Actually, a lot has changed, wouldn't you say?"

Erika had no answer. At least not one she wanted to give. Teri had hit the proverbial nail on the head. A lot had changed. At the same time, nothing had changed. Chase still didn't believe in marriage. And even if he did, Erika wouldn't hurt her family by marrying a man they hated.

****

"Hey, do you have a bike?"

Erika looked up from the magazine when Chase walked out onto the patio. She hadn't really been reading it.

After lunch with Teri she'd spent the rest of the morning at Louise's helping to get things ready for the twins' upcoming birthday party. Lauren had spent most of the time complaining about Chase. Erika had spent half the time reining in the impulse to defend him, and half the time wondering why he was being so stubborn and wouldn't let Lauren have the girls Friday night. Was it really such a big deal? Couldn't he live without them for one night?

Which meant she'd spent all of her time feeling torn in two. "What?" She forced away her troubled thoughts and focused on Chase.

"Do you have a bike?" he repeated.

"Yeah, I have one in the garage. I haven't ridden in ages, though. Why?"

Chase pulled out the chair across from her and sat down. He wiped his forehead with the back of his hand. "I thought maybe I'd cut out of here early today. We

155

could throw the bikes into the back of my truck and head down to the lake."

She frowned. "Knock off early? You took the whole day off earlier this week because we—" She stopped. "I am on a deadline here, Chase. The repairs need to be done by a certain date."

His brow furrowed at her tone. "I'm well aware of your deadline, Erika. Things are going really well. We're ahead of schedule. I thought it would be fun to spend some time together outside of the house."

He looked at her, but she couldn't quite meet his gaze. The fresh layer of guilt she'd acquired at Louise's today weighed heavily on her.

"Is something wrong?" he asked after the silence had grown too long to be comfortable.

"No. Why would anything be wrong?" She took a sip of water. Would he notice how her hand trembled?

He studied her, a thoughtful look on his face.

"What?"

"Spend some time with Louise and Lauren today?" His light, casual tone sounded forced.

She set the glass on the table with a little more force than necessary. Water sloshed over the side. "What is that supposed to mean?"

He leaned back in his chair and folded his arms across his chest. "You tell me."

"Look, I'm not in the mood for your games right now."

He laughed, but the sound held little amusement. "You sound just like her."

"Like who?" She mimicked his pose, arms crossed in front of her.

"Lauren."

She opened her mouth then pressed her lips firmly together. It did sound like something her sister-in-law would say. Especially to Chase. "Very funny."

"No, I'm serious. Whenever you spend time with the family, you act differently around me."

She looked away, unable to meet his eyes any longer. "I don't know what you mean."

"I think you do." His chair scraped across the pavers as he pushed it back. He disappeared around the side of the house.

She dropped her head into the cradle of her arms. What a fine mess she'd made of things. Fighting with Chase didn't help matters. Maybe they should end the relationship before someone got hurt. Him. Her. Her family.

Unfortunately, she had a sneaking suspicion quitting Chase wouldn't be easy. Especially cold turkey. Like a junkie, she could only go so long before she needed a hit. Hopefully in time, the overwhelming craving for him would lessen, then cease all together.

In the meantime, she owed him an apology.

She found him out front, sanding the boards on the new porch. His hand moved in rhythmic circles on the rough wood. "Chase?"

He looked up. She sat on the top step. "I'm sorry." She laid a hand on his arm to still its motion. He brushed his hands off then sat down next to her. She leaned her head on his shoulder. "I shouldn't have snapped at you."

"I thought you were okay with all this. With the way things are between us."

"I thought I was, too. I am." She sighed. She'd made her bed, now she needed to lie in it. Of course, lying in it with Chase was all too appealing and made her forget all the reasons she shouldn't be doing what she was doing in the first place. She shook her head to clear its convoluted musings. "You were right. I was at Louise's today. She's still so sad about Kevin. If she knew I'd gotten involved with someone else so soon it would be awful for her. And if she knew it was you, she'd be devastated."

"I'm so sorry. I know how hard this is on you. I never should have asked you out. I never should have…" His lips brushed her hair. "Maybe it would be best if we didn't see each other any more."

The words cut into her. The pain prompted her quick denial. "No." She pulled away to look at him.

Chase raised an eyebrow.

"I mean, I know it's selfish, and I know if we continue this, there's a big chance we're going to get caught. Someone's going to get hurt. But…"

"But?"

She hid her face in his shoulder again. "I'm not done with you yet," she mumbled.

His laughter vibrated through her. "Well, I guess I'm glad to hear that." He sobered. "I wish this wasn't so hard on you." He hesitated. "Will you promise me something?"

"Sure."

"When you're not okay with all of this, when you're through with me"—she heard the smile in his voice—"be honest. Tell me. I promise I'll accept your decision. Will you do that for me?"

She nodded and drew herself up. "You're too good to me, Chase. I promise. Like I said before, I'm a big girl. I know what I'm doing."

Being near Chase made the guilt seem less heavy. Easier to bear. Mostly because her overwhelming need for him overshadowed everything else. She needed another hit, and soon. After all, the sooner she got him out of her system, the better. Then she could move on with her life. "So, is your offer for a bike ride by the lake still open?"

He studied her, looked like he wanted to say something, but changed his mind. "Sure, the offer's still open." He gestured to the porch. "I need to finish sanding this and put one coat of sealer on. It'll take me another hour or so, and then that's all I can do for the day anyhow. The first coat needs to dry before I can put another one on tomorrow."

"Perfect." She kissed him on the cheek then rose. She brushed the back of her shorts off. "I'll pack us something to eat. Let me know when you're ready."

****

Cycling down by the lakeshore proved to be a pleasant outing. No worries about being seen with Chase. Erika couldn't remember the last time Frank or Louise or Lauren had been downtown. The soft, albeit warm, breeze off of the water. A blue cloudless sky arching overhead.

They stopped for ice cream at a stand in the park. Laying their bikes on the grass, they sat with their backs against a thick tree trunk.

The creamy, strawberry treat slid down Erika's parched throat. The cool shade was a welcome relief from the hot sun pouring down on her while riding. Even the breeze generated by the movement of the bike couldn't compete with the almost 90 degree day.

After enjoying the last crunch of the sugar cone,

she sighed in contentment. "Ah. That hit the spot."

"Yep." Chase closed his eyes and leaned his head against the bark.

His strong profile contrasted with the soft curve of lashes against his cheek. The easy rise and fall of his chest as he breathed deeply caused a hitch in her stomach. Well-muscled, tanned legs dusted with fine, dark hair brought erotic memories. Her heart pitter-patted. Of course he was even more amazing beneath the physical features that attracted her to him. The love he showered on his daughters. The care and attention to detail he put forth in his work. His sense of humor. His strength of character.

He really would make a good husband. Despite the way his marriage to Lauren had turned out and his subsequent views on marriage, maybe someday he'd reconsider. A man like Chase shouldn't be alone. He should be loved. And love someone in return.

"So you really don't ever want to get married again?"

He opened one eye. If the out-of-the-blue question surprised him, his expression didn't show it. "Nope. Why? Were you planning on proposing?"

"No, silly." She smacked his arm. Although a tiny thrill ran through her. What would it be like to be married to Chase? To be Erika Stewart. Her name. Her life. Joined with his. She buried the fantasy deep in her subconscious. No use even fantasizing about the impossible.

"You should though, you know." Both eyes open now, he stared at her, his expression enigmatic.

"Should what?"

"Get married again."

She hugged her knees to her chest. "Maybe someday. When enough time has passed." When Louise could handle it. When Erika's love for Chase faded. She glanced at him. Would it ever?

The more time they spent together the deeper her feelings grew. Another reason she couldn't let their so-called fling go on much longer.

"Is Kevin's family always going to dictate your life?"

She stiffened. "They're my family, too."

He sighed. "I know. I just don't think you should let your dead husband's mother and sister dictate any part of your life."

She didn't answer. Although he claimed to understand, how could Chase really know how important Kevin's family was to her? He'd never known what it was like to not have one. He had a father, mother, a sister, and, of course the girls. They were bonded together by blood and love.

Her blood family had never really cared about her. But Kevin's had. Lauren really was like a sister.

"You know what's ironic?"

"What?"

"I think Lauren would be okay with it."

"With what?"

"With me getting married again." She glanced over at him. "Not to you of course." Even if Chase wanted to get married again, Lauren wouldn't be *that* understanding. "But the other day she offered to set me up with someone from Jim's office."

Chase plucked a blade of grass and wound it around his finger. "Why did you say no?"

"What makes you think I said no?"

His startled gaze met hers.

She laughed. "I'm just kidding. Of course I said no."

"Why?"

Because some nameless, faceless businessman from Jim's office held no interest for her. She wasn't interested in any man but Chase. Of course she couldn't say that. Not when she'd promised him a no-strings-attached summer fling. So she shrugged. "Louise kind of freaked out when Lauren mentioned it, so nothing came of it."

"See what I mean?"

"About what?"

"About Louise dictating your love life."

"It's not like that."

Chase frowned, but didn't comment again.

"How would you feel if Lauren got married again?"

"I'd be happy for her." He glanced at her. "Do you think she will?"

"I don't know for sure, but I think she's getting pretty serious with Jim." Chase held less animosity toward Lauren than she held for him, so his sentiment was probably true, but how would Chase feel about the girls having a stepfather? A man who would, based on the custody arrangements, see the twins more than Chase did.

Would it improve his relationship with Lauren if she married Jim? Or make it worse?

Even though he was a temporary part of Erika's life, she wanted him to be happy. Even after they went their separate ways and went back to being nothing more than former in-laws, seeing each other from time to time at family events, a piece of him would always remain in her heart.

****

On the way home, Chase looked over at her and smiled. "Want to have a sleepover at my house?"

"Yes." Erika didn't even have to think about it. An excited buzz droned though her at the thought of being tangled up with Chase in the sheets of his bed. In fact, she'd packed a small overnight bag in hopes of an invitation.

However, when they arrived at Chase's place, much to her surprise and chagrin, a more practical matter took precedence over her need. The afternoon in the hot sun had left her looking and feeling like a damp dishrag.

As soon as they walked in the door, in sync with her thoughts as always, Chase turned to her. "Okay, first things first. Showers?"

"Oh, God, yes."

He grinned. "Okay. Do you want to go first, or should I?" He stepped closer. His voice lowered. "Or do you want to share?"

Declining the tempting offer made testament to how gross she actually was. Plus, she needed to shave her legs. Definitely not romantic or sexy. "Why don't you go first?"

He looked down at himself, then back up at her and raised an eyebrow. "That bad, huh?"

She laughed. "No offense."

Chase finished quickly then showed her where to find a towel and other necessary items. After showering she pulled on a T-shirt and shorts, and then padded barefoot down the hall to the living room.

Chase closed his book and looked up at her. "Squeaky clean?"

She nodded. "I feel much better. A little less like a dirty dishrag."

"Good." His glance swept over her. "Hey, you're bleeding."

"Darn it, I must have cut myself shaving." She dabbed at the thin trickle of blood on her knee.

Chase rose. "Let me get you a Band-Aid." He disappeared down the hall but returned shortly and held out the bandage.

She pulled the wrapper off. "I should have known." The smiling face of the Little Mermaid looked out at her.

He shrugged. "Sorry, it's all we have."

"I love it." She secured the adhesive in place over the small cut.

"Do you want me to kiss it and make it all better?" The child-like reassurance contrasted with the husky note in his voice.

Anticipation curled through her. With the shower out of the way, she could focus on a more pressing priority. Chase. "Definitely."

"Come here, then." He tugged her to the couch. He sat and settled her legs over his. He smoothed his hand down her thigh, then around to the back of her knee. Goosebumps peppered her skin. He traced his finger around the Band-Aid before lowering his head to feather his lips across the plastic strip.

"Ah," she murmured. "It's all better now."

"Amazing, isn't it?" He toyed with the damp hair falling over her shoulder. It curled around his finger. "Can I do something?"

"What do you want to do?" A rhetorical question. As long as he didn't stop touching her, she'd let him do whatever he wanted.

"Come sit on the floor in front of me."

She complied and looked up at him expectantly.

"No, with your back to me."

She turned and settled between his legs. He lifted a section of her hair and let the strands sift through his fingers. She sighed as a delicious shiver slid down her spine. He combed through the damp strands then separated it into three sections. With deft motions, he twisted the sections together into a braid.

"I braid the girls' hair all the time," he murmured as he worked. "Yours is thicker, heavier." He lifted the woven strands as if weighing them. He draped the long rope of hair over her shoulder, then leaned down and kissed the side of her neck. "Do I ever braid your hair in your dreams?" he whispered.

"No," she managed. His lips moved along her throat, making speaking difficult.

"Hmmn? Something we haven't gotten to yet. Maybe you'll dream about it tonight?"

"Actually, since I've experienced the real thing, my dreams have kind of paled in comparison."

"Ah, you flatter me." He turned her around and lifted her onto his lap so she straddled his hips. His hands spanned the bare skin at her waist beneath the hem of her T-shirt. His thumb brushed her navel.

She bunched the fabric of his shirt in her hands and tugged it up, then over his head. Her palms skimmed the firm muscles in his chest. Her fingers trailed across his ribs. His stomach tensed.

He threaded his fingers beneath the plait on the

back of her head. With gentle insistence, he applied pressure until her mouth lowered onto his. His head fell back to rest on the cushions as she raised herself on her knees to align her mouth more perfectly with his. His tongue scraped across hers in a slow, sensuous dance.

Deep in the pit of her stomach, sparks of desire flickered. She ground against the thrust of his erection. His hands found her hips, not to still the motion, but to hold her in place. The persistent tingle between her thighs intensified, demanding his attention.

His mouth left hers to bestow nibbling kisses along the underside of her jaw. "In your dreams, do one or both of us ever have too many clothes on?" He whispered the words in her ear then gently bit the lobe.

A shudder wracked her. "S-sometimes. But we have a lot of fun remedying the situation." She gave him a wicked smile.

His hands dropped from her waist. "Be my guest." The fire in his eyes singed her. The heat settled in her womb.

Never taking her gaze from his, she stroked down his chest, following the dark trail of hair bisecting his firm stomach until it disappeared into the loose waistband. Her thumbs caught the elastic and eased it down to reveal the ridges of his hipbones.

She licked her lips in anticipation of lowering the straining fabric an inch or two further. His hips lifted, encouraging her to slide the shorts off. She stopped and pressed a soft kiss to his lips. Moving no more than a millimeter away, she whispered, "On second thought, maybe I'll go first."

His lips quirked beneath hers. "Tease."

"I prefer to think of it as setting the mood." She

primly pushed off his lap to stand in front of him. With slow deliberation, she inched up the hem of her T-shirt. When she bared her breasts, Chase's breath hissed out from between his teeth. She yanked the shirt over her head and dropped it to the floor.

She eased the elastic waistband of her shorts down to her hips then paused. Tilting her head to the side, she regarded him. "Hmm? Now we match…"

"Keep going," Chase growled.

"Impatient, aren't we?"

"You have no idea. Keep going." His velvet tone softened the demand.

She sent him what she hoped was a sultry stare and wriggled out of the shorts. They pooled at her feet. She kicked them aside.

He groaned, but managed a half smile. "So, now there's only one problem."

"A problem?"

His gaze swept over her naked body. The flames in the dark depths of his eyes blazed brighter. "We don't match anymore."

"An easy fix." She knelt on the couch, one leg on either side of his.

She reached for the tie on his shorts, but his hands on her waist stopped her and eased her onto her back. His breath stirred the curls in the juncture of her thighs as he pressed a kiss right below her navel. He moved lower until his lips brushed the silky hair.

Her head fell back. "If you keep distracting me, we'll never match." Her voice shook.

"I'm making sure we match everywhere. As you can see," he gestured toward his arousal, "I'm more than ready for you. Are you ready for me?" He slid a finger into her slick warmth.

She bucked against his hand. Shivers raced through her. She trembled.

In desperation, she ripped the shorts down his legs. He kicked them off. She grabbed them from the floor.

"No pockets," she panted.

"On the end table."

She found the square packet, tore it open, and rolled the protective sheath on him. The room spun as he flipped her onto her back into the cushions of the couch and plunged into her in the same movement. Tiny explosions peppered her from head to toe, centering where he filled her with his hard, pulsing need.

Her back arched and he took the opportunity to lower his head and suck a nipple into his mouth. He tugged rhythmically in time with the thrust of his hips. She burst apart as he buried himself deep inside her with one final push.

Minutes—or was it hours?—later, she became aware of her surroundings. The soft cushions behind her back. The erotic press of Chase's weight. He shifted so they lay on their sides facing each other on the narrow couch.

She ducked her head and tucked it under his chin. "I'm in trouble," she murmured against his throat.

"Trouble?"

"I think I'm addicted to you. Like a junkie needs his crack."

His laugh rumbled through her. "You make it sound like a bad thing?"

"It is. Addictions only get worse over time. And I need to give you up soon. Summer's almost over." The thought stole some of the light from her afterglow.

He didn't answer right away. Instead, he pulled her closer and kissed the top of her head. "Don't worry," he said finally. "We'll figure it out."

****

Would they figure it out? The thought ran through Chase's mind later as he lay entwined with Erika in the twisted sheets of his bed.

They'd known having a relationship would be complicated. Erika's summer fling label had seemed perfect at the time. A little fun. A little pleasure. No strings attached. Break the rules for a while and no one would be the wiser.

Erika's admission about being addicted to him had struck a chord. He could relate, because he felt the same way. He'd promised he'd accept her decision when she decided to end things, and he would. But it wouldn't be easy.

They were connected. The connection had always been there. Not in the sexually aware way it was now, but even back when they were merely in-laws. Back when things had been simpler, they'd always understood each other. Had been able to relate to one another on a level different than simply family members.

Over the last few weeks, the connection had changed. Grown stronger. Deeper. Only part of it centered around sexual attraction. Much more about Erika attracted him. Her innate goodness. Her loyalty and commitment to her family. The joy she found in the little things.

He was dangerously close to offering her something he never thought he'd offer another woman again. Something she couldn't, or wouldn't, accept even if he asked.

He wanted to share his life with her. And it scared the living hell out of him.

Chapter Twelve

"I think Chase is seeing someone."

Lauren's out-of-the-blue comment made Erika choke on a sip of water.

"Are you okay?" Lauren asked.

"Fine," Erika gasped, trying to catch her breath. The two women sat in the kitchen at Louise's house making final preparations for the birthday party.

"What makes you say that?" Louise asked from her position in front of the sink.

Erika held the breath she finally managed to catch.

Lauren shrugged. "I'm not sure. It's only a hunch. Little things I've noticed lately. Like when I called over there a few weeks ago he was talking to someone in the background. And I called pretty early. He just seems…happier."

Erika ducked her head, hoping no one would notice the guilt surely etched on her face. The warm, cozy feeling of knowing she made Chase happy warred with gut-clenching worry. Beneath the table, she pressed her knees together to stop her legs from trembling.

"What in the world did you call over there for?" Luckily Louise's thoughts were elsewhere, and she didn't seem to notice Erika's discomfort.

"Remember? I wanted to keep the girls last night so they'd be here early for the party."

Remember? How could they forget? Lauren harped

about it all morning on Wednesday.

"I thought if I asked him far enough in advance, he wouldn't have a problem with it, but of course he refused. Like I knew he would. He's so impossible sometimes."

Erika almost jumped in to defend Chase, but stopped herself just in time. She snapped her mouth closed and focused on the faux wood grain of the table in front of her.

"You should know better." Louise brought a plate of rolls over and set them in front of Erika. "Would you cut these, honey?"

Erika mumbled in the affirmative.

Louise turned her attention back to Lauren. "Think of it as another reminder why you divorced the man."

Although the disparaging comments about Chase were nothing new, Erika bristled at the conversation. She had always taken Lauren's comments about her ex-husband with a grain of salt, but had sympathized with her plight. Now she found her loyalties swaying in the other direction. Chase wasn't the monster Lauren made him out to be.

The Chase Lauren talked about and the Chase Erika had fallen in love with almost seemed like two different people. Lauren perceived Chase as an unyielding, stubborn, unworthy man, while Erika saw him as tender and caring and giving. No one who loved his children as much as he did could be as unfeeling as Lauren made him sound. Even if they weren't married anymore, why couldn't Lauren see those traits in him? Didn't she know Chase at all? Anyone who saw him with the twins could never accuse him of being anything but a loving, devoted father.

Could Erika's feelings be blinding her from seeing the true Chase? Could she be missing something Lauren saw? No, even Lauren admitted Chase was a good father. Her issues with him were solely personal.

Today Lauren seemed even more irritated with Chase than usual. Probably because she hadn't gotten her way about keeping the girls last night. Best to just ignore the extra snippiness.

"Well, I really don't care who he's sleeping with. If getting some helps improve his attitude and outlook on life, then all the better. But he'd better not be doing it when my children are around."

The crude comment snapped Erika out of her reverie. Lauren had crossed from snippy to downright rude. Her nasty tone snaked down Erika's spine. How could anyone talk so cruelly about someone they used to love? It offended her to have her relationship with Chase relegated to something so vulgar as "getting some." Then again, maybe Lauren's comment hit too close to home. After all, what had she promised him all along? Nothing more than a quick summer fling. No pressure. No strings. No commitment.

Besides, Lauren spent time with Jim when the girls were around. Erika would bet her next paycheck he spent the night sometimes. Talk about a double standard. Guilt followed closely on the heels of indignation when she glanced at Louise. Her mother-in-law had always been so good to her. What would she say if she ever found out what Erika had done?

"Well, honey," Louise said to Lauren. "You know how men like Chase are. They can't be satisfied without a woman."

Erika pondered the untruth in the words. Before

her, Chase had been completely satisfied without a woman. He didn't want or need a woman in his life. He had his girls. They were enough for him. So why *had* he gotten involved with her?

She sighed. Probably for the same reason she'd gotten involved with him. Perhaps Lauren hadn't been far off the mark. To "get some" seemed like a good enough reason as any. Erika winced. It sounded so sordid.

Lauren harrumphed and went to the sink to wash her hands. "Enough about him." She wiped her hands on a towel as if wiping Chase out of her mind. "I'm going to see what Jim and Dad are doing downstairs." She strode from the room.

Silence fell. Louise seemed preoccupied with dinner preparations, which gave Erika more time to think. Too much time. Why *had* she gotten involved with Chase? With someone who couldn't offer her a future? Not that it mattered. Even if he could offer a future, she couldn't accept it. Too much stood in their way. Maybe she needed to accept the fling had run its course. No good would come of it if she and Chase continued their dangerous game. Too many people stood to be hurt.

Better to end it now, go cold turkey, before things got really out of hand. He'd simply be her carpenter. After he completed the work at her place, he'd return to being her former brother-in-law.

It sounded so simple in her head. So rational. So easy. But it made her heart ache to think about not being with Chase any more. To never feel the whisper of his fingers on her bare skin. To never taste the heady flavor of his kisses.

In time the incessant desire for him would cease. Wouldn't it? The gnawing ache of withdrawal wouldn't last forever. The memory of their stolen time would fade. She'd forget how his kisses made her tingle all over. She'd forget how the heat from his body spread from his to hers when they lay together in the rumpled sheets of her bed. Or his. She'd forget how he made her happier than she'd been in a long while. She'd forget how much she loved him.

She'd forget it all. Or die trying.

She squared her shoulders, strengthening her resolve. Her summer fling had come to an end. Time to accept it and move on. All she needed to do now was tell Chase. Telling him would be the easy part. Forgetting would be difficult. But she'd find a way. She had to.

The front door opened, admitting two giggling four-almost-five-year olds and their father. Erika's heart knocked against her ribs.

"Hi, Grandma!"

"Hi, Aunt Erika!"

The girls rushed to embrace Louise and Erika as they walked out of the kitchen. Chase stepped into the foyer looking as if he'd rather be anywhere else in the world. Her heart went out to him. She barely curbed the impulse to go to him. Wrap her arms around him. Comfort him.

His gaze met hers. Her stoic resolve of moments earlier melted, replaced by a hot rush of need. Intimate secrets danced within the dark orbs. A guilty blush warmed her cheeks. Would everyone else be able to see those secrets, too? They fairly burned her with their intensity.

Okay, so maybe telling him wouldn't be so easy.

"Hello, Chase."

"Hello, Louise." Chase pulled his scorching gaze from Erika to address his former mother-in-law. "How have you been?"

"Fine. Yourself?"

She gritted her teeth at the forced pleasantries. She hated it when they acted this way. More so now. It was like being trapped between two opposing forces. Trapped between love for her family and desire for a man they hated.

The tension thickened as an awkward silence fell. Matters didn't improve when Lauren entered the room. Jim and Frank followed. "Chase."

"Lauren." He glanced down at his watch. "Two minutes ahead of schedule." Mockery laced his voice.

Erika frowned. She expected catty behavior from Lauren, not him.

Lauren's eyes narrowed. "Good for you." She turned her attention to the girls. "Hi, sweeties."

"Hi, Mommy." The girls' greetings were restrained, as if they could sense the animosity between the adults. They pressed close to Chase, eyes wide, uncertain.

Chase's gaze shifted to Jim.

Erika couldn't help but compare the two men. Both were tall, they stood eye-to-eye, but any similarity ended there. Chase's dark hair fell over his forehead in unkempt, casual disarray. He sported a dark blue short-sleeved polo shirt and khaki shorts, which enhanced the laid-back look. On the other hand, Jim kept his blond hair shorter, more styled. His button-down shirt and pressed slacks had a formal, business-like air about them. How could Lauren have fallen for two such completely different men?

Jim held out his hand. "Jim Harrison."

Chase took the proffered hand. "Chase Stewart."

Jim nodded. "Nice to meet you. I've heard a lot about you."

Chase's gaze returned to Lauren. "I'm sure you have."

Lauren rolled her eyes.

Needing to escape the suffocating hostility, Erika turned her attention to the girls. "Want to come look at your birthday cake?"

Squeals of excitement greeted her comment, and Steph and Sami each grabbed one of her hands.

"Is it chocolate?"

"Does it have the Little Mermaid on it?"

Erika let their exuberance wash over her. It took the edge off the tension permeating her body. "I guess we'll have to see, won't we?" With a quick glance at Chase, she led them away.

****

Later, Erika found herself out on the deck with Chase and Frank.

Frank turned from the grill. "Where'd everyone go?"

"Inside, getting the rest of the food ready."

"Do you need any help, Frank?" Chase asked.

"No, no. I've got it. You sit and relax." He waved the barbeque tongs in Erika's direction. "Erika's having some work done over at her place, Chase. Maybe you know her contractor."

Erika choked on her soda. Her eyes met Chase's then darted away.

"Maybe I do." His calm voice held no trace of the panic clawing at her insides.

"Who's your contractor, Erika? Chase can let you know if the guy's any good or not."

Had Frank always been so persistent? "Um." Why couldn't she recall the name of one of the other contractors who had given her a bid? "Dave…" Oh what the hell was his last name?

"Robinson," Chase supplied.

She flashed him a grateful smile when Frank turned back to the grill.

"Dave Robinson," he continued. "He's a fabulous contractor. You can't go wrong hiring him."

"Yeah, um, things are really coming along. The windows and painting are done, and the front porch is nearly finished." At last, something she didn't have to lie about.

Frank nodded. He looked over at Chase. "It's a shame she didn't think of hiring you."

Erika's eyes bugged. If she'd known her family would be accepting of Chase as her contractor, she could have saved herself a lot of agony and guilt. Then again, Frank always had shown less animosity toward Chase than Lauren and Louise.

Chase's gaze found hers again. His eyes twinkled, but his face wore an I-told-you-so expression. "Yeah, too bad we didn't think of that."

She made a face at him behind Frank's back.

Before the conversation could deteriorate further, the screen door scraped open. The twins bounded out, followed by Lauren and Jim. Steph scampered over to Chase and leaned against his knee. "Daddy, I'm hungry."

"It's almost time to eat."

"I'm hungry now."

He ruffled her hair. "I'm sure you are, but you need to be patient a little bit longer."

Her face settled into a pout.

"How much longer?" Sami joined in.

"About fifteen minutes," Lauren supplied. "But first I want to take some pictures."

"Aw, do we hafta?" Steph whined.

"Yes, you have to. Birthday pictures are part of the birthday party."

Sami made a face. "Rats."

Erika smiled at their disgruntled expressions.

Lauren grabbed her camera from the table. "Okay, how about one in front of the flowers over there?" She pointed.

With matching sighs, the girls trudged over to stand in front of the flowerbed. They soon forgot all about their reluctance as they posed and preened for the camera, each trying to outdo her sibling. Their similar white sundresses stood out in front of the colorful blooms comprising the backdrop. Their dimpled smiles tugged at Erika's heart. They looked so like Chase when they grinned.

Lauren turned to Erika. "Would you take one of the three of us?" She knelt on the ground between the girls. She wrapped an arm around each of their waists. They squeezed in on either side. Erika snapped off a few pictures.

"Jim, I want one with you in it, too."

Erika's glance darted to Chase. A muscle worked in his jaw as the other man went over to join the trio. Jim scooted in next to Lauren and put his arm around

Sami. Erika risked another look at Chase. He sat rigid in his chair. His hands gripped the plastic arms so tightly his knuckles turned white. Her heart ached for him. Seeing his precious children with another man in a cozy family scene was the cruelest kind of torture. His gaze met hers. The ache in his eyes matched the one in her heart.

"Erika?"

She tore her gaze from Chase and turned to Lauren. "What?"

"The picture?"

"Oh, right." She peered at the digital screen and took the photo as quickly as possible.

"Aunt Erika, you be in a picture now."

Jim stepped aside so Erika could take his place. She knelt and pulled Sami closer. The little girl leaned against her and put her hand on her knee.

"Hey, you have a Little Mermaid Band-Aid. We have ones just like that at Daddy's."

Erika's heart lodged somewhere in her throat. With a Herculean effort, she kept her gaze from once again seeking out Chase. Would anyone else discern the hidden meaning behind the innocent comment? Would they figure out she'd gotten the bandage at Chase's house?

When no one reacted, she slowly expelled the breath from her lungs, but her heart continued to race.

"Now Daddy, you get in a picture," Sami instructed.

Lauren grimaced as Chase sauntered over. Erika rose.

"No, with Aunt Erika, too."

It took a while longer and lots of trading places

with various people moving in and out, but eventually the girls tired of posing. "Can we eat now?" Steph demanded.

"Yes, we can eat now." Frank removed the hotdogs from the grill and put them on a serving plate.

"Yippie!" Sami shouted.

Although the food, abundant enough to feed a small army with enough leftovers to last a week, smelled delicious, Erika didn't have much of an appetite. She sat as far away as possible from Chase, but physical distance couldn't erase the overwhelming awareness that hummed through her in his presence.

Could everyone else sense it? How could they not know she'd been intimate with him? The evidence, mixed with a large dose of guilt, must be visible on her face every time she accidentally glanced at him. Which happened far too often for her own peace of mind.

After dinner, somehow she wound up clearing dishes from the buffet table with him. She yanked her arm away when it accidentally brushed his.

He raised an eyebrow. All he said was, "Interesting party."

"You could say that." She glanced over his shoulder to where Frank stood talking to Lauren.

Chase's gaze followed hers. "Afraid they'll kick you out of the family for talking to me?"

She blinked, his words coming too close to the truth for comfort. The caught in the middle feeling intensified. "Look, Lauren's really on the warpath about you today, and I don't want to make things worse."

He waved his hand in a dismissive gesture. "She's pissed because she didn't get her way about keeping the girls last night."

"Exactly. And if she sees us talking…"

"Dammit, Erika. Don't let them do this to you. There's no reason we can't talk to each other here. Be friends."

She stacked the empty potato salad bowl on top of the serving platter in her hand. The ceramic rattled together. "Is that what we are?"

"Aren't we?"

She didn't answer.

He leaned closer. The woodsy scent of his aftershave drifted over her. She closed herself to the memories it evoked. Now wasn't the time for an erotic daydream.

"I mean, obviously, there's more between us. But here, in this place, there's no reason we can't be friends."

"I can think of a lot of reasons." She peered over his shoulder again. Would the rest of the family think they'd been talking too long? Or was she being paranoid?

"Why don't we tell them I've been working at your place?"

"Are you crazy?" she hissed.

He shrugged. "I don't think it would be such a big deal. Frank kind of gave it his blessing."

"Chase, please. You can't be serious."

His eyes narrowed. "What if I am? It's not like I'm suggesting we tell them we're sleeping together."

The plates lurched in her hands. "Would you keep your voice down?" She rebalanced the dishes and avoided his gaze. "Maybe it would be best if you didn't work at my house anymore."

"What?"

She risked a glance at him. The look in his eyes matched the dangerous tone of his voice.

"Are you firing me or breaking up with me?"

"I really don't think this is the best place to talk about it." Her gaze darted over to Frank and Lauren again.

"The hell it isn't." Chase glanced over his shoulder. He turned back to her and took the dishes from her hand. They clattered onto the table. He grabbed her arm.

"What are you doing?" Erika gasped in alarm as he led her around the side of the house. "What if someone sees us?"

"I don't give a damn."

She probably deserved his anger, but self-preservation kicked in. A touch of panic stabbed into her. She only wanted to protect herself and her family. Being alone with Chase was dangerous. "Let me go." She yanked her arm, but his grip held firm.

"Not until you answer my question."

She looked up at him. Then away. "I don't know. Maybe both."

He swore beneath his breath. "Why?" He bit the word out.

She sighed. "You know why."

He let go of her and folded his arms over his chest. "Explain it to me again."

She glanced behind him. Would someone notice they were gone? She nibbled her fingernail. "Please. Not here."

He ran his fingers through his hair. "Okay. Fine. Not here. But we're going to talk about this," he warned.

She swallowed. "Yes." They definitely needed to talk. But not here.

He looked at her for a long moment. She tried not to squirm. "I-I need to go back. I need to finish with those dishes." She inched around him, half afraid he'd stop her again.

He let her go.

****

Erika hurried away.

"Dammit." Chase slammed his fist against the side of the house, welcoming the abrasion of the rough brick against his skin.

Bearing the guilt of their relationship was hard for Erika. He understood and didn't judge her for it, but he wanted her to be able to talk to him without that haunted look in her eyes.

He rubbed his hand over his face. Maybe it would be best if they went their separate ways. Their relationship wasn't going anywhere. It couldn't. Why prolong the inevitable? They'd known it couldn't last. What had Erika called it? A summer fling. Well, summer was almost over. Time to move on.

He'd find someone to finish the work he started at her house. Why make things more awkward than they needed to be? If they were going to end things, might as well make a total break. He promised her he'd accept her decision to end things when the time came. He just never thought it would be so soon.

A dull ache throbbed through him. He couldn't imagine not seeing her again. But he had to do what was best for her. If it cost him a small piece of himself, he'd gladly sacrifice it if it meant she wouldn't hurt anymore.

"Daddy, we've been lookin' all over for you." Steph's singsong voice interrupted his troubled thoughts.

"We're gonna cut the cake," Sami added.

"Mommy says we'll do it without you if you don't hurry up."

He frowned, not in the mood to deal with Lauren's snide comments. Especially when she made them to his daughters. "She's only teasing," he lied. He refused to stoop to his ex-wife's level and make disparaging remarks about her to the girls.

"C'mon. Let's go cut that cake." He headed back to the patio, the comfort of a small hand tucked into each of his.

Chapter Thirteen

She had to end things with Chase. Pain ripped through Erika at the thought, even though it was the right thing to do. She couldn't take being torn in two anymore.

Monday when he came over to work, she'd tell him. The cowardly part of her considered calling him after the girls went to sleep, but she dismissed the thought as soon as it formed. He deserved better.

Would he keep his promise and accept that she'd decided to end it? Of course he would. He was honest. Honorable. Decent. Which made the whole thing even harder to bear.

Sunday slipped by slowly as she had nothing to look forward to but the unpleasant task ahead. What would she say? What would he say? Would she be able to get through it without crying? She'd spent a lot of time this summer crying all over Chase, maybe she could find the strength to spare him one last bout.

Late in the afternoon, Teri called. She wanted to stop by in the afternoon the next day to pick up some plans for a unit they'd been working on for the fall. It didn't take her long to pick up on Erika's melancholy mood. "Hey, you okay?"

"I don't know."

"Chase?"

Erika sighed. Teri was nothing if not perceptive.

Usually hashing out the dismal details of her life with her best friend helped her gain some perspective. Today she didn't feel like it.

True to form, Teri didn't push. "If you want to talk, you know where to find me."

"Thanks."

The day dragged on, but conversely, night arrived all too soon. Erika had no desire to wake up in the morning to face a new day. A day when she needed to tell Chase goodbye. And mean it.

Of course morning arrived right on schedule. She glared toward the sound of birds chirping through the open window. How could anything be cheerful on a day like today?

Chase arrived as she was finishing her morning coffee. She hadn't attempted anything else, afraid it wouldn't stay down. He took one look at her face and sighed. "Yeah, I thought it might be like this."

Determined to be strong, she swallowed the lump of tears in her throat. "I'm sorry. I can't do this anymore. I thought I could handle this. But then the birthday party…" Her voice cracked, but her gaze never strayed from his.

"I know." The soft note of compassion and understanding in his voice threatened to undo her. "I never meant for any of this to happen."

"I'm not blaming you."

"I know that, too." He smiled, but it was the saddest thing she'd ever seen.

Her heart broke. She hugged herself and looked around, unable to bear looking at him anymore. The kitchen taunted her with memories. When he'd come over telling her he wanted to help her out. When they'd kissed for the first time. When they'd shared a kiss before their first date.

Forgetting wouldn't be easy.

Chase pulled a folded piece of paper from his back pocket. "I, uh, kind of thought this might be where we were heading, so I brought you the name of someone who can finish up your porch." His lips quirked into a humorless half-smile. "I figured it might be…easier if I didn't stick around even to work."

Conflicting emotions tore at her. Surprise at the thoughtfulness of the gesture. Relief he'd accepted her decision so easily. Agony at the thought of not seeing him any more.

Erika took the paper. She yanked her hand away when their fingers brushed. She still wanted him with a desperate, yearning need. To quell the impulse to reach out to him, she jammed her hands into her back pockets.

He took a step closer and cupped the back of her head in one hand. He leaned down and brushed a kiss across her forehead. "Goodbye, Erika." He turned away. Panic flooded through her. Was it really going to end like this? Without one last touch? One last kiss?

In the doorway, he pivoted to face her. His lips quirked again in the same, sad smile. A piece chipped out of her heart. "Look, I promised I would accept it when you ended things. And I will, I swear. But does it have to be like this? Can't we have a proper goodbye?"

"A proper goodbye?"

He walked toward her with slow deliberation. "You know, break the rules, one more time." His hand stroked down her cheek.

The rational part of her warned her one more time

for old time's sake would be the worst idea in a long line of bad ideas. Best to quit now while she was somewhat ahead. While part of her heart remained intact. But Erika's flesh had warmed from his touch, and already shivers of anticipation rippled through her. The addicted part of her begged for one more hit.

She wavered.

Seeming to sense her indecision, Chase pressed his case by brushing his lips over hers. Logic and common sense lost ground. When his mouth opened over hers, and he deepened the kiss, her resolve crumbled.

What would it matter if they broke the rules one last time?

She wrapped her arms around his neck, pulling him down so she could return the fervent kiss. The erotic sound of their harsh breathing echoed off the hardwood floor and granite counters.

In the past their lovemaking had been sensual and heated, but now a primal, desperate need drove Erika. Eager for the touch of his flesh against her own, she yanked his shirt over his head, while he undid the buttons of her sleeveless blouse. In their haste, her clumsy fingers fumbled with the buckle of his belt.

His more competent hands brushed hers aside. He yanked the leather through the loops then dropped it to the floor with a soft clank. The snap of his jeans proved easier to deal with, and soon he'd shucked those as well. She kicked her shorts out of the way, and then finally they stood facing each other, naked, in her kitchen.

She shoved all emotion aside and opened herself to fully concentrate on her body's physical reactions. Her heart pounded. Her breath escaped in short gasps. Her legs trembled. Damp heat pooled between her thighs.

Chase's pupils dilated. His chest rose and fell with the harsh cadence of his breath. His arousal thrust toward her. He put his arms around her and they melted to the floor in a tangled pile of limbs. His lips took hers in a passionate, wet, open-mouthed kiss. Desire, raw and fierce, consumed her. Her nails raked his back.

"My wallet," he ground out.

She scrabbled around on the floor, snagged the leg of his jeans, and dragged them toward her. He wrenched the wallet out of the back pocket then tossed it aside after retrieving the square packet.

Her legs cradled his thighs, and she wrapped one foot around the back of his knee as he entered her with a smooth, easy flex of his hips. He remained still for long, delicious moments before he moved inside of her. He pushed in then pulled out, setting a rhythm to match the frantic beating of their hearts.

When she shattered, she closed her eyes to savor the moment. Brilliant flashes of light lit the dark behind her lids. Chase shifted, rolling her on top of him as he thrust up one final time. His hands grasped her hips, holding her to him as he found his shuddering release.

Erika eased off him and lay on her back on the hard floor. She stared at the whirring ceiling fan as her heartbeat and breathing gradually returned to normal. In the small space between them, he reached for her hand and entwined their fingers. She twisted her head to look over at him.

He smiled, but his eyes remained serious. "Are you mad at me?"

She frowned. "Why would I be mad at you?"

"For talking you into breaking the rules one more

time."

Her lips twitched. "I don't recall a whole lot of talking."

"True."

"No, I'm not mad." How could she be? She hadn't fought very hard. Had she fought at all? "This was perfect."

"Good."

They moved the goodbye party to the bedroom, then early in the afternoon to the couch. Afterwards, Erika snuggled next to him under a light blanket, memorizing the feel of his arms around her, the whisper of his breath stirring her hair, the steady beat of his heart beneath her ear. Tomorrow—tonight—she'd have nothing but the memories to hold close.

The doorbell pealed, breaking the cozy silence. Erika glanced at the clock. Drat. Teri was early.

"Expecting someone?" Chase queried.

She pushed away from him, ignoring the sting of separation, and rose from the couch. She wrapped the blanket around herself. "Teri's stopping by to pick up some papers." Her glance slid over his body. "Go put your pants on." Regret laced her voice.

"Yes, ma'am." He sauntered toward the kitchen.

She took a moment to admire his naked backside then went to open the door. "Sorry, Teri, I—" The words lodged in her throat.

"Hi, Erika," Lauren said. "I know I usually don't stop by unannounced like this, but I hoped you had a minute. I really need to talk to you about something."

Erika's heart beat so fast she thought Lauren would be able to hear it. She pulled the blanket tighter around her shoulders.

"Look, this isn't really a good time. I…"

Lauren's gaze swept over Erika's attire. "Oh, I'm sorry, were you sleeping?"

Erika gritted her teeth. "No, I…that is, I was, uh, relaxing with a book. The air conditioning. It was chilly in here…" Her lame excuse trailed off.

"Oh, I—" A noise from the kitchen drew her attention.

Erika cursed to herself. Panic made her pulse sprint. What was Chase doing in there? She prayed whatever it was kept him occupied. Had he heard Lauren's voice? Would he know not to come out into the foyer?

"Is someone else here?"

"Uh, no, I…" She glanced over her shoulder and sent a telepathic message to Chase. *Stay in the kitchen.*

Lauren's eyes widened in understanding. "Oh."

Erika hurried to explain. "It's not what you think, but now isn't really the best time. Why don't I call you later?" She inched toward the door, hoping Lauren would take the hint. She had to get her out of there.

"You don't have to explain. I know Mom's been giving you a hard time lately, but I think it's great you're moving on with your life."

"You do?" Surprise momentarily overrode her panic.

"Yes, I do. And don't worry, I won't tell—" She broke off as her eyes widened in shock.

"Sorry to interrupt, I—" Chase's words choked off abruptly. "Lauren."

Erika wished a hole would open and swallow her. She wished she could turn back time. She wished she were anywhere but standing in her foyer between Chase and his ex-wife wearing nothing but a blanket. Risking a glance over her shoulder, she stifled a groan. Chase had donned his jeans, but they were unbuttoned. His chest was bare.

Before Erika could say anything, Lauren turned to her. Her mouth opened, but no words came out.

"Please let me—" Erika began.

"You're sleeping with Chase?" The words, when they finally came, held a note of incredulity.

A cold shiver snaked through Erika and she hugged herself.

"It's not what you think," Chase said.

"Oh, really?" Lauren raised a disbelieving eyebrow.

"Look…" Erika tried again.

"How long has this been going on? Were you two sleeping together when we were married? When Erika was married to my brother?"

Erika reeled back in shock, astonished at the accusation. "Of course not. How could you think that?"

"You're out of line, Lauren," Chase said.

"*I'm* out of line? I think you have it backwards." She looked from Erika to Chase once again. "I can't believe this," she said almost to herself. Her gaze focused on Chase. "I suspected you were seeing someone but I never dreamed…" Her accusatory glance landed on Erika. "How could you do this? You're like my sister." She turned to go.

"Wait," Erika said. "Please let me explain."

Lauren's gaze flicked from her to Chase once again. "I don't think you can." She paused with her hand on the doorknob. "And I think it would be best if you didn't come to Mom's birthday party next week."

The door closed behind her with a soft finality.

Erika's heart cracked. She turned to face Chase, then found she couldn't look at him.

"Come here." He drew her into his arms.

But the comfort she had once found there had disappeared. Now only the pain of heartbreak remained. She pulled away to move into the living room. She stood in front of the fireplace, not really seeing it. What had she done? His hands fell on her shoulders. She shrugged away and crossed her arms over her chest, unable to bear the guilt of his touch.

He shoved his hands in the front pockets of his jeans and regarded her with regret filled eyes. "I'm sorry."

She shook her head. "You don't have anything to be sorry for. This is all my fault."

"No, it's not. If I had left this morning instead of talking you into…"

She smiled sadly. "You didn't talk me into anything. I wanted it as much as you did." She turned away. "It doesn't matter now. What's done is done. I knew going into this what I was doing was wrong. And I did it anyway. I went in with both eyes open, knowing I'd have to face the consequences of my actions one way or another. I guess you could say I'm getting what I deserve." The calm words gave no indication of the gaping wound in her bruised and battered heart.

"Erika."

"I think you should go now."

He left the room. She gave him a few minutes then followed him into the kitchen. He stood by the patio door, fully dressed, looking out over the backyard. He turned at her approach, but remained silent.

"It, uh, would be best if you didn't call me." She avoided looking at him. "I'm hoping someday they'll be able to forgive me, and I want to be able to go back to them with a clear conscience…no more lies. I want to honestly be able to say it's over between us and I haven't talked to you."

He reached for her. She took a step back. "Don't. Please don't…touch me." She didn't have the strength to endure it. "I'm sorry I dragged you into this. I know it's already difficult for you, dealing with Lauren, and now I've made it worse."

"I'll manage." His voice sounded odd.

"Of course." The inane platitude sounded ridiculous, but what else could she say?

"Give Jeff a call. He'll finish the porch for you."

"Right." Repairs on the house were the last thing on her mind. How would she repair her heart? The pain of losing Chase knifed into her. The loss of her family hurt just as much. She couldn't have them both, so she had to let him go.

The crack in her heart split wide and flooded her chest with agony as he walked out the door.

****

A week later Chase sat in the living room with the twins watching their favorite movie. Concentrating on the screen proved difficult, and not because he'd seen the movie at least a million times. The movie reminded him of Erika.

"Can't we watch something else for a change?" he asked when he couldn't take any more. The singing crab brought back vivid memories of kissing Erika. He remembered the taste of her, the feel of her beneath him. He stifled his groan.

He'd respected her wishes and hadn't called. But it hadn't stopped him from thinking about her during every waking moment.

"But, Daddy, this is the best part," Steph protested.

Sami turned tear-filled eyes on him.

He cursed silently. His voice must have been harsher than he intended. He didn't want to take his heartache out on the girls. "I'm sorry, moppets. Of course we can watch this."

"Why did you sound mad?"

He grimaced. "I'm not mad. I-I was thinking about something else."

Steph nodded wisely. "I was mad the other day when Aunt Erika didn't come to Grandma's birthday party."

Chase didn't want to pursue the topic, so he nodded in return. But true to her five-year-old personality, his daughter wasn't easily dissuaded. "I think Grandma's mad at Aunt Erika about something."

How much did the girls know about the situation? He gave in and asked, "Why would she be mad at her?"

"I heard her tell Mommy Aunt Erika shouldn't come to dinner anymore," Sami piped in.

Chase cursed again under his breath. Couldn't Lauren keep her conversations private? The twins didn't need to be in the middle of this particular family squabble.

"I like Aunt Erika."

"Me, too."

"Daddy, do you like Aunt Erika?"

How in the world should he answer? "Yes, I do." Those simple words hid a rainbow of emotions. Emotions he wasn't ready to analyze because liking didn't come close to describing how he felt about Erika.

"Can she come to dinner here?"

He whipped his head around. "Um, I don't think that's such a good idea, honey."

"Why not?"

He gritted his teeth at their tenacity. "Um, well, Aunt Erika is very sad right now, and she needs to be by herself."

"Oh."

"But when I'm sad I like to be with you."

"Well—" Thankfully the doorbell saved him from needing to respond. "Your mom's here."

Steph raced to answer the door, but Sami paused, looking at him with eyes that somehow seemed older than her five years. "I love you, Daddy."

"I love you, too, sweetie," he said around the lump in his throat. He pulled her into his arms. "Thank you," he whispered in her hair.

"Chase."

He looked up at the sound of Lauren's voice. "Lauren." He rose from the couch and set Sami on her feet.

He studied his ex-wife, trying to read her thoughts, but her eyes revealed nothing. She'd conveniently been on the phone when he picked up the girls on Friday, so they hadn't talked since the incident at Erika's.

She turned to Sami and Steph. "Go get your things. I need to talk to your father."

The twins hurried to their bedroom.

"You look like hell."

His gaze snapped back to Lauren. "What?"

Hers wandered over his face, taking in the dark patches under his eyes and the shadow of stubble on his jaw. He did look like hell. Sleepless nights did that to a person.

"Have you talked to her?"

He narrowed his eyes. What was she up to? He shook his head. "No."

"What's going on between you two?"

"Nothing."

"Nothing? Come on Chase, I'm not stupid. I was there, remember?"

How could he forget? "I was doing some construction work for her. We spent a lot of time together, talking and catching up, and then we went out a couple of times. We're not seeing each other any more."

"Seeing each other? Is that what you call it?"

"I'm really not in the mood to talk about this right now." Especially with her.

She ignored him. "Why aren't you seeing each other any more?"

"Why do you think?" Impatience laced his voice. "Look, not that it matters, but it was over when you…found out."

"It didn't look over to me. Or do you always walk around your customers' houses with your shirt off?"

He ignored the snide comment. "Erika couldn't stand the guilt of lying to her family."

"What about you?" Lauren sounded more thoughtful than angry.

"What about me?"

"How do you feel?"

"About lying to your family?" He quirked an eyebrow. "It doesn't bother me."

Amazingly, Lauren smiled. "Ha ha. No, I meant

how do you feel about Erika ending things?"

"I accepted her decision. Our relationship wasn't going anywhere. Like I said, she couldn't take the guilt and I...well, even if the family wasn't an issue, I don't believe in permanent relationships." Why was he explaining himself? Especially to his ex. It wasn't any of her damn business.

She folded her arms over her chest. "Are you still hung up on your whole marriage-is-crap thing?"

He raised an eyebrow.

Lauren sighed. A disgusted look crossed her face. "Really?" she demanded.

He held onto his temper with effort. Who was she to judge? "Let's look at a few examples, shall we? How about if we start with us?" He jabbed his finger between the two of them.

Lauren snorted. "Bad example."

"My point exactly."

"That's not what I mean. We started out all wrong. We didn't have a chance in hell from the beginning." She gave him a shrewd look. "Tell me something. When we got married, did you love me?"

His mouth dropped open. He closed it with a snap. "What kind of question is that?"

She smiled. "Just answer it. Honestly."

He huffed out a breath. "Honestly, huh? Then, no," he said softly. He didn't want to hurt her, but she deserved the truth.

"See what I mean? We got married for all the wrong reasons. We weren't in love with each other. But you're in love with Erika."

"I can't be in love with Erika." The denial sounded weak even to his ears.

"Why not?"

"I…" He faltered and groped for words. "I can't offer her anything. I have the girls. They're my life."

"I know you love Sami and Steph. Everyone knows that. But don't you want someone to share your life with? Erika would make a great stepmom. Why does it have to be an either/or kind of thing? You can love the girls and Erika at the same time you know. It's two completely different things."

Surprise rendered him mute. Lauren actually sounded supportive. She had to have an ulterior motive. Didn't she? "Why are you fighting for this so hard? Do you want me to be with Erika? I would have thought it would be the last thing in the world you'd want, let alone try to talk me into."

She looked away. "I know it seems strange, but I want her to be happy. I really do think of her as a sister. And you make her happy. In the last couple of months she's been happier than I've seen her since my idiot brother started cheating on her."

Chase's head snapped up.

"Oh, yeah, I knew." Lauren shook her head. "Or at least suspected."

"You never said anything to anyone?" Anger tinged his voice.

"As a matter of fact I confronted him about it. I told him to get his head out of his ass. Erika didn't deserve to be treated like that. I told him he needed to come clean with her, or else I would tell her myself." Her voice grew sad. "But then he was killed. I don't think he ever did tell her."

"She knew."

Lauren's expression grew pained. She muttered an

unfavorable comment about Kevin under her breath. Then she straightened. "But this isn't about Kevin. It's about Erika. She's happy now. Or at least she was until…" She winced, but continued, "And you." She gave him a sly smile. "You're happier, too. Happier than you've been since before we got married."

He shook his head. "I don't think—"

"You know I'm right. Don't argue with me about this."

For a moment Chase let himself get lost in the fantasy of loving Erika. Of being a family with her and the girls. But then the fantasy crumbled. Her family would never accept him.

He voiced the thought aloud. "Your family would accept me as a part of her life?"

"Yes."

He snorted. "Oh really? When's the last time Louise talked to her?"

Lauren lowered her eyes. "It was hard on Mom, finding out you and Erika are…together."

Chase bit back a retort. Lauren had been the source of information. If she hadn't told Louise, Erika wouldn't be ostracized from her family. Then again, if he hadn't given into his baser desires, none of this would have happened either. Pointing fingers wouldn't fix things.

As if reading his mind, Lauren sighed and met his gaze again. "I'm sure my reaction didn't help, but you have to understand how shocked I was to see you at her house like…like that. I had the feeling you'd been seeing someone, but to find out it was Erika…"

Chase blew out a breath. He did understand. "I know."

"It took me a while, but after I calmed down and thought about it, I realized you two actually make sense together. More than you and I ever did. But to answer your question, yes, I think Mom can accept you in Erika's life. She loves Erika. She'll see how happy you make her." She laughed self-consciously. "You've been the bad guy in Mom's eyes for a while now."

He rolled his eyes.

"My fault, I know. It'll take some time, but she'll get used to you as the good guy."

"You have a lot more confidence than I do. I don't want Erika to be hurt again. She's been through enough."

"I agree. Which means the ball's in your court now. *You* have to decide if you want a future with her. Everything else will work itself out."

Chase fell silent and contemplated her words. Could she be right? Did he and Erika have a chance? *Would* everything work out?

Lauren glanced at her watch. "Shoot, I have to go. I was supposed to meet Jim half an hour ago. Sami. Steph," she called. "We need to get going."

They came into the living room, identical pouts on their faces. "Do we hafta? We didn't finish our movie with Daddy."

He hunkered down in front of them. "We'll finish it next week."

"Promise?" Sami asked.

"Promise," Chase echoed.

"Cross your heart and stick a needle in your eye?" Steph prodded.

He shook his head. Where did they learn those things? But he smiled and pantomimed the requested gestures.

They threw their arms around his neck. "Yippie."

"I love you, Daddy," Sami said.

"Me too, me too, me too," Steph joined in.

He squeezed them to his chest and closed his eyes. "I love you, too. I'll miss you." Then he rose and placed a hand on either of their shoulders. "Do you have your backpacks?"

"Yep."

They grabbed their bags from next to the door. Each, of course, bore an identical decal of their favorite mermaid. To avoid confusion, each girl's name had been embroidered on the flap of their respective pack.

"All set?" Lauren had watched the usual goodbye scene with an unusual amount of patience.

"Yep." With a last hug to Chase's legs, the girls headed out.

Lauren turned at the door. "Think about what we talked about. About what you want. About how you feel. But I'll tell you this, if you let Erika go, you're a bigger idiot than my brother."

Later, Chase lay awake and mulled over Lauren's words. How in the world could his ex-wife be the voice of wisdom in all of this?

Erika would never believe it either.

What in the world had happened to change Lauren's attitude?

And was he really ready to offer Erika what she deserved—a husband who would cherish her until the day he died. Could he be the one?

****

After a busy week, he hadn't gotten any closer to answering the questions rioting through his mind than he'd been since he talked to Lauren. Friday after work, he stopped for a coffee on the way home to clear his head. On his way into the shop, he ran into Dave Robinson.

"Chase, how's it going?"

"Fine," Chase lied.

"Hey, how'd that job go? The one for your sister-in-law or someone?"

Chase fought back a grimace. "The job went fine." Much of the rest of his life had fallen apart, but Erika's porch and windows had turned out well. "Speaking of which, I have a job lead I want to pass along to you. You know, for letting me underbid you on the other one."

Dave shook his head. "You don't need to do that."

"I want to. I really appreciated it. I have the information at home. I'll give you a call later this week."

"Okay, sounds good." Dave glanced at his watch. "I have to get a move on. I have a date with my wife tonight."

"A date?"

Dave chuckled. "Yeah, we try to get out of the house a couple times a month and have a night to ourselves. No kids."

"How many kids do you have now? Two? Three?"

"Three and another on the way."

"Congratulations, man." Chase held out his hand.

Dave shook it. "Thanks."

"So, date nights, huh? That works for you guys?"

"Like a charm."

"You don't mind leaving the kids with a babysitter?"

If Dave thought the question strange, he didn't show it. "Hell no. Like I said, it gives Jennie and me a little time alone."

"Well, then, I won't keep you," Chase said. "I'll be in touch later this week with the information on that job. Have fun on your date."

"Oh, I plan to." Dave laughed. "See you around."

"You bet."

Chase pondered their conversation while he fixed his coffee. Easy sugar, easy cream. Maybe it was possible to have it all. Kids and a happy marriage. With Erika. Ironically the place to start would be to break his promise to her. They needed to talk.

Chapter Fourteen

"Hello?" Erika barely recognized the dull lifeless voice as her own when she answered the phone. She'd ignored its persistent ring the first time. And the second. But when it pealed for the third time in less than a half hour, she picked it up. She'd long ago given up the hope of hearing Chase's voice on the other end of the line. She had no business wanting him to call. She told him not to. And he'd respected her wishes.

So of course she shouldn't expect it to be him. Still, she couldn't stop the little stab of disappointment each time she picked up the phone and didn't hear his voice.

Or Louise's. She hadn't spoken to her mother-in-law in weeks. Louise had made it very clear she didn't want to hear from Erika. No surprise there.

She'd lost everything. Chase. Her family.

So hearing Lauren on the other end of the line took her completely by surprise. "Erika? Thank God I finally got hold of you."

"Lauren?" It took a moment to process the urgent note in her sister-in-law's voice. "What's going on? What's wrong?"

"It's Dad."

Erika's heart stalled. Her grip on the phone tightened. "Wh-what happened? An accident?" The memory of the phone call she received about Kevin flooded through her. Her weak knees gave out and she sank onto the couch.

"No." She paused. "They think he had a heart attack."

"Oh my God. Is he…" She couldn't say the word.

Lauren read her mind. "No, no, he's going to be okay."

"How's Mo…Louise?"

"She's doing okay. Shocked. Scared. But doing better since the doctor said Dad was awake and responsive."

Erika closed her eyes and sent up a silent prayer of thanksgiving. Then horror replaced her relief. Stress caused heart attacks. *She'd* caused a lot of stress in Frank's life recently. It was her fault.

"What do you mean your fault?"

Had she spoken aloud? She swallowed. "It's my fault this happened."

Lauren still sounded puzzled. "How can this be your fault?"

"Because of Ch-Chase." Saying his name was difficult. "About what happened between us." How would Lauren react to the reminder of her and Chase's indiscretion?

She swore Lauren snorted. "Erika, this wasn't your fault. What happened with you and Chase didn't have anything to do with Dad's health issues. I'd say the three-egg omelet he has every morning was more of a culprit than anything. We've all been after him for years to watch what he eats. He never listened."

The explanation did little to reassure Erika. "How did it happen?"

"He and Mom were eating lunch. Dad said he

didn't feel well. Got short of breath and said his left arm felt kind of numb, so Mom called an ambulance. The doctors think he had a mild form of cardiac arrest. They're keeping him overnight for observation, but he should be able to go home tomorrow, or Monday at the latest."

"Well, that's good news." She hesitated. "Thank you. For calling me."

"I thought you'd want to know." Lauren paused. "He's over at Northwest Community. I'm sure he'd like to see you."

Erika's breath caught. A spark of hope filled her chest, but reality quickly extinguished it. Frank might like to see her, but Louise sure wouldn't. "I-I don't know if that's such a good idea. I mean, Mom— Louise—might not be so thrilled if I show up."

"Actually, I think it would mean a lot to her if you did. She misses you."

Erika's heart skipped a beat.

"Dad's on the second floor, by the way," Lauren added.

"Are you sure? I don't want to do anything else to upset him. Or her."

"You're part of this family, Erika. I know things have been strained lately, but we still love you."

Tears welled in Erika's eyes. She cleared her throat. "Thank you. That means a lot."

"Well it's true." She paused. "Has Chase called?"

"No. Why would he? I told you, we're not...seeing each other anymore." With everything going on, Erika's love life was sure to be the last thing on Louise's mind. But maybe when things calmed down, Lauren would mention it.

"Oh." The other woman's voice sounded odd. "Impossible man," she muttered. "So stubborn."

"What?"

"Nothing I—Wait, hold on. What?" she said to someone at her end. "Oh, okay. Erika? I have to go. We'll see you soon, okay?"

Erika disconnected the phone. Conflicting emotions roiled through her. Relief Frank would be okay. Guilt, because despite Lauren's claims to the contrary, she couldn't help but feel responsible for what had happened. Indecision: she wanted to see Frank to assure herself he really was all right, but still worried how Louise would react.

The fact Lauren had called at all said something. Maybe Erika could mend fences with her family. Maybe they'd all be able to put the past behind them and move forward. Especially if she assured them Chase was not a part of her life anymore and never would be. If they forgave her, she'd have to avoid any kind of contact with him at all. On the rare occasions he'd be around with the twins, she'd make sure she wasn't there.

In time, maybe they'd be able to see one another at occasional family gatherings again. Eventually things would go back to normal. She'd be Chase's former sister-in-law. The way it should have stayed all along before she'd thrown all her rules, along with her common sense, out the window and gotten involved with him.

Right now it hurt too much to think about seeing him. The memories of their time together were too fresh. The consequences still weighed heavily in her heart.

She ignored the insistent voice in the back of her head telling her a life without Chase wasn't much of a life at all. But life with him wasn't an option. The thing she needed to focus on was getting her family back. Going to see Frank in the hospital seemed like a good place to start.

Forty-five minutes later, she stepped off the elevator on the second floor at the hospital. Trepidation swirled in her stomach. Combined with the antiseptic and medicinal smell, it made her slightly nauseous. She spotted everyone immediately at the end of the hall. With a deep breath, she walked forward.

Louise sat in a chair. Across from her, Jim and Lauren huddled together on a green couch. Louise glanced up as Erika approached. She looked haggard and tired. Older than the last time Erika had seen her. A tiny frown marred her features. Erika's heart sank. She almost turned around.

Lauren followed Louise's gaze. She rose and hugged Erika. "You came."

Erika nodded. Lauren seemed genuinely pleased to see her.

Louise turned to Lauren. "You called her?"

"Of course."

Louise studied Erika, but didn't comment.

"Erika." Jim rose to greet her with an awkward one-armed half-hug. "It's nice to see you."

"You, too."

He resumed his seat next to Lauren and took her hand.

An uncomfortable silence fell. Erika shifted from one foot to another. She chewed a fingernail. "How's Frank doing?"

"The doctor's in with him right now," Lauren replied.

"He should be out any minute," Louise added, but avoided looking directly at Erika.

"Oh, okay. Do-do you mind if I wait with you?"

"Of course not. Have a seat." Lauren motioned to the chair next to Louise.

Erika took the proffered seat, but didn't relax back into the vinyl cushions. She sat stiffly, knees pressed together, and hugged herself.

Louise kept her eyes fixed on the clock on the wall at the far end of the hallway. Lauren and Jim had their heads close together, murmuring in quiet conversation. A stab of envy pierced Erika. She longed for the comfort of someone's arms around her. Chase's arms.

She forced the thought away. She shouldn't be thinking about him. Especially now, being here with her family once again. This is where she wanted to be. Even if the palpable tension in the air threatened to choke her, this is where she belonged. With her family.

She blew out a breath. Her gaze flicked to the clock. What was taking the doctor so long? Shouldn't he have come out by now? Maybe Frank's condition had worsened.

Finally, after what seemed like hours, the doctor approached from the corridor to the right. In unison, they rose. Lauren huddled close to Jim. He put his arm around her shoulders.

"Doctor, how is Frank?" Louise spoke first. Her voice shook.

Erika curbed the impulse to take Louise's hand, unsure the other woman would welcome the gesture.

"He's doing fine," the doctor assured her. "Keeps

saying he wants to go home," he added with a smile.

Louise sagged with relief. "That sounds like Frank."

The doctor noticed Erika for the first time. "Hello, I don't believe we've met. I'm Doctor Adams." He held out his hand.

Erika shook his hand. "Hello, I'm Erika."

"Erika is our daughter-in-law," Louise said.

"Nice to meet you, Erika."

Erika nodded, but couldn't return the pleasantry. Not with her heart lodged up in her throat. Not only had Louise not told her to get the hell out, she'd even called her daughter-in-law. She swallowed back tears.

"So, what's the prognosis, Doctor?" Lauren asked.

"Frank is going to be fine. We'd like to keep him overnight, and he'll need to set up a series of follow-up appointments with his regular physician. He'll probably put him on a special heart diet."

"Of course," Louise said.

"His cholesterol levels are pretty high, so the first priority will be bringing those down."

Erika nibbled a fingernail then asked the question burning in her mind. "You think those high levels caused the heart attack? Not stress or something else?"

Louise turned to her, her mouth open in surprise, but the doctor spoke before she could. "To be honest, after looking at his levels, I'm surprised something like this didn't happen sooner. I think this incident should be taken as a wake-up call. A very serious one. Frank needs to monitor his health very closely from now on, starting with what he eats."

Louise nodded. "Oh, he will. I'll make sure of it."

Dr. Adams smiled. "Excellent."

"Can we see him now?" Lauren asked.

"The nurse is finishing up, but then you can go in. Maybe only a couple of you at a time. He's awake, but I want him to get as much rest as possible, so if he seems tired, let him sleep."

"Of course." Lauren nodded.

"Now, if you'll excuse me," Dr. Adams said. "I need to check on another patient. I'll be back around later tonight to check on Frank again."

"Thank you, Doctor," Louise said.

After he'd gone, Lauren put her arms around Louise. "See? He's going to be okay."

Louise sniffed and wiped a tear from her cheek. "I know." She laughed, but it sounded shaky. "I've been telling him for years to watch what he eats."

"Well, now he's going to need to listen." Lauren glanced down the hall. "Do you want a cup of coffee or something while we wait for the nurse to be done?"

"No, I'm fine. I—" Louise cut herself off as the elevator dinged. She looked toward the sound. Her lips thinned. "What's he doing here?"

"Erika."

At the sound of Chase's voice, Erika turned so fast the walls blurred around her. Her pulse raced and her mouth went dry. She swallowed. "Ch-Chase. What are you doing here?" Her question echoed Louise's. No wonder her mother-in-law hadn't looked pleased.

"I called him."

Erika turned to Lauren in surprise, but before she could say anything, Louise spoke. "Why?"

"To let him know about Dad." She turned to Erika. "I figured you wouldn't call him." She added something under her breath that sounded like, "As

213

stubborn as he is."

Chase's mouth quirked. Erika couldn't fathom what could be even remotely funny at a time like this.

She stood rooted to the spot, unable to take her eyes off of him. Indecision warred inside her. She longed to be wrapped in his arms to find the comfort only he could give. But Louise's censuring gaze held her back.

After weeks of heartache, she'd finally made progress with putting things right with her family. She couldn't throw it all away for a few minutes of comfort. She had to be strong. So she wrapped her arms around her waist, hugging herself, to avoid temptation.

Chase stared back, his expression now serious and his eyes filled with sympathy and a touch of uncertainty. Something else flickered in them as well.

Too many emotions flooded through her. Worry over Frank. Surprise at Lauren's gesture. The ache of seeing Chase again. The see-saw events of the last hour and a half overwhelmed her.

To suddenly be here with her family. And Chase. After not hearing from either of them for weeks.

Although the lonely silences had come about because of her fling with Chase, there was one big difference. Her family hadn't called because they were angry with her. Chase hadn't called because she'd asked him not to.

But today he'd come. For her.

"Erika." The tender care and concern in his voice curled into her heart.

Her resolved wavered. She took a step toward him. He held out his arms. The temptation of the comfort she'd find there proved too much to resist. And her aching heart, for once and for all, took a side. For better or worse. Come what may. "Oh, Chase." Her voice trembled.

He closed the distance between them and pulled her into his embrace. She buried her face in his neck, inhaling the familiar scent of his aftershave. His deep sigh vibrated through her as his arms tightened. "How's Frank?" he asked finally.

"He's going to be fine," Lauren answered.

"It's all my fault," Erika murmured.

"What?" A chorus of voices reacted.

"Because of what I did. With you. Because of us Frank is in here."

Chase set her away from him. He held her upper arms and looked into her eyes. "What are you talking about? Who told you that?" His gaze flicked over her head.

"N-no one. I just know."

"Sweetheart, it's not your fault."

"Chase is right."

Everyone turned to look at Louise.

Erika stared at her mother-in-law in shock. Had she actually agreed with Chase?

Louise squared her shoulders. "Frank's heart attack had nothing to do with you…and…" She faltered then gathered herself, "Chase. You heard what the doctor said. His diet caused this. Nothing else."

"Mom's right," Lauren added. "You know we've been telling him for years to change how he eats. It finally caught up with him."

Before Erika could argue further, the nurse walked out of Frank's room. She approached Louise. "You can go in now if you'd like."

Louise nodded. She started down the hall then turned. She gazed at Erika, and then at Chase, who had his arm around her. She straightened her shoulders. "Thank you for coming, Chase."

Erika stared after her, her mouth open in surprise. Finally she snapped it closed and looked up at Chase. His bemused expression mirrored her confusion.

"Yes, Chase, thank you for coming." Lauren looked at Erika, a small smile on her face. "I thought you would."

"Thank you for calling." Chase turned to Jim and held out his free hand. "Jim."

Jim returned the gesture. "Chase."

Erika shook her head to corral her tangled thoughts. But before she could, Lauren spoke again. "Where are the girls?"

"Mrs. Fremont from next door came over to watch them."

It took a minute for the words to sink in. When they did, Erika whirled to face Chase. "You left the girls with a babysitter? To come here?"

His brow furrowed. "Yeah." His voice held a question.

"But why?"

His puzzled frown deepened. He gestured with his hand. "This isn't really the place for them."

"But you came." Her voice trembled with emotion. "Yes."

"You never leave the girls with a sitter."

He still seemed confused by her train of thought. "Hardly ever, but I thought you might need a shoulder to lean on. I hoped you wouldn't need it to cry on."

Erika made an effort to assimilate Chase's words,

but no matter how she tried, she couldn't wrap her head around them. He'd left the girls at home to come be with her? She shook her head. "But, they're the most important thing in the world to you. Nothing...no one...else is as important to you as they are."

Understanding dawned in his eyes. He took her hands in his as he looked deeply into her eyes. Her breath caught at the emotion shimmering in his. "My girls are two of the most important people in my life, but Erika, you're right at the top of the list, too." He smiled.

Her heart melted.

"Sweetheart, there's room in my life for all of you. If you want to be in my life." He quirked an eyebrow. "Because, remember, if nothing else, I am good for a shoulder to cry on now and again."

Erika swallowed before she was able to reply. "You're good for a lot more than that." They stared at one another until Lauren discreetly cleared her throat. Erika jumped.

"It seems like you two have a lot to talk about," Lauren continued. "It's about time," she added under her breath.

"Yes, we do," Chase said. The look in his eyes made Erika's insides turn to mush.

"Well, then, I guess Jim and I will go check on Dad."

Erika barely noticed their departure.

Chase smiled the smile she loved. Her tummy flipped over. He took her hand and tugged her closer. "I've missed you." His gaze flickered around the waiting area before returning to hers. Before she could do more than catch her breath at the look in his eyes, he ducked his head to press his lips to hers.

The kiss was brief, but tender.

She burrowed against him and tucked her head into his shoulder. The familiar comfort of his arms was like coming home. She sighed in contentment. She'd missed him, too. She didn't want to ruin the sweet flavor of their reunion, but she'd be a fool to think all of their problems were over and they could walk off into the sunset together.

"So, what happens now?" She leaned slightly away in order to look up at him.

He touched a finger to the tip of her nose. "So it seems we're done hiding from the family?"

She hesitated. Her family had accepted Chase's presence at the hospital better than she ever dreamed possible. Lauren had been the one to call him in the first place, and Louise had thanked him for coming. Definitely a step in the right direction.

"Yes." She wouldn't keep any more secrets from them, but whether or not they'd accept Chase in her life was a whole different matter.

"Good," Chase said simply. "Then Lauren is right. We have a lot to talk about."

She nodded. Her family played only a part in their complicated relationship. Chase had said he wanted her to be in his life. But what did he really mean? By his own admission, he didn't want to get married again.

She looked around. The small waiting area was empty, but doctors and nurses bustled through the halls. Patients shuffled along the corridor. "This probably isn't the best place to talk."

"No, probably not."

"I don't want to leave until I see Frank."

"Of course not. We can—"

"I don't mean to interrupt," Louise's voice broke in.

Erika turned to face her mother-in-law. Louise's gaze fell on Chase's arm around her shoulders and lingered for a moment, but she didn't comment.

"You can see Frank now, if you'd like."

Erika nodded. She stepped away from Chase, but squeezed his hand. "I'll be right back."

"Both of you can go." Louise paused and looked at Chase. Erika couldn't read her expression. She didn't look angry, though. "I'm sure Frank would like to see you, too, Chase."

Erika's mouth dropped open. She closed it with an almost audible snap. Had she fallen into some alternate universe?

"Thank you." He turned to her. "Do you mind if I come with you?"

Although her head spun, she managed a semi-coherent answer. "O-of course not." She glanced over her shoulder at Louise as they walked toward Frank's room. Her mother-in-law offered a half-smile.

Erika pulled a deep, albeit shaky, breath into her lungs to stave off the tears before entering Frank's room. He looked up from his hospital bed as they walked in. His gaze hovered on her and Chase's joined hands before he met hers. Something like satisfaction lit his eyes.

She swallowed. "Hey, Dad. How are you feeling?" Several tubes snaked from his arm into IV bags next to the bed. A myriad of screens hung above his head. The steady blip of the heart monitor reassured her.

Frank grimaced. "Fit as a fiddle, but they won't let

me out of here." He motioned to the equipment around him. "Got me hooked up to all these contraptions so I can't make a run for it."

Overwhelmed at seeing him look and sound so well when she'd expected the worst, Erika forced back her tears and smiled.

Frank's glance moved over to Chase. "Chase. Good to see you."

"You, too, Frank."

Frank's gaze dropped once again to their joined hands. She fought the urge to pull away from Chase. For better or worse, she was done with the lies. As if reading her thoughts, Chase tightened his fingers around hers.

"So, you two are done keeping secrets?"

She gasped. Had Frank read her mind, too? But Chase's voice sounded calm as he replied, "Apparently we weren't very good at it."

Frank's lips twitched, but his eyes remained serious as he regarded them. Finally he nodded. "It's definitely not the worst thing that's ever happened to this family...us finding out."

"Dad, I'm so sor—"

Frank held up the hand not attached to wires. "I'm not looking for an apology. And on that note, what's this nonsense about you thinking you're the reason I'm in here?"

She gasped again. "Lauren told you what I said?"

"Actually, Louise did."

Words escaped her, but Frank continued before she needed to say anything. "Y'all have been telling me for years I need to watch what I eat. I was too stubborn to listen, so I don't want to hear anymore of this blame stuff, got it?"

"Got it." The words were meek.

"Anyway, like I was saying. I'm not sorry we found out about you two. I am sorry you felt the need to hide from us in the first place. I guess while we are talking about blame, it lies with a lot of people in this case. But I hope all the lies and blame are behind us now. You two can move on with your lives."

Could they? Louise hadn't thrown her out of the hospital, but it didn't mean she was as ready to accept Chase in Erika's life as Frank was. Besides, she still wasn't quite sure exactly how Chase would fit in her life, or rather, how she would fit in his.

Frank looked at Chase. He gave a wry smile. "Hell if I thought I'd be asking you this question again, but are you going to marry my girl?" He inclined his head toward Erika.

She blanched. "Dad…" She and Chase still had a lot to discuss about the future. What he'd told her earlier about wanting her in his life didn't mean he'd changed his mind about marriage. "It's not like that. We—"

Chase squeezed her hand. His eyes remained on hers as he answered Frank's question. "Yes, sir, I am."

Chapter Fifteen

"Thanks for being so nice to Frank. I'm sure what you said back there made him happy." Erika attempted to sound nonchalant as they walked down the hospital corridor. After Chase's heart-stopping announcement, and Frank's nod of approval, they stayed only a few more moments before making their excuses to leave so he could get some rest.

Chase raised an eyebrow.

She chewed her fingernail. She wanted him to know she hadn't taken his response about getting married too seriously. He'd made his view of marriage perfectly clear. She had to find a way to reassure him she hadn't taken his words as any kind of proposal.

She looked up at him while they strolled down the hall. "You know, about getting married and all." Her gaze darted away. "I'm sure it made him feel better. It was nice of you to be so kind to him."

He grasped her arm to halt her progress. "You think I was just being nice to Frank when I said I planned to marry you?" His voice sounded odd.

"Well, yes...I mean, I know how you feel about marriage and..." Her gaze bounced around to look at the walls, the floor, and the food cart in the hallway. "I want you to know I understand and I—"

He muttered a curse under his breath and grabbed her upper arms. "Erika. Stop." The frustration in his eyes matched the tone of his voice. "For your information I wasn't just being nice to Frank. I—" He glanced around. "I really don't want to have this conversation here." He looked at her for the space of several long heartbeats. "Come have dinner with the girls and me tonight."

Her heart thudded in her chest, but she shook her head. "Oh, I couldn't. I don't want to intrude on your time with them."

A rueful smile curved his lips. "You're not listening to me, are you?" His teasing tone took the sting out of the words. He tucked a strand of hair behind her ear and ran his fingers down her cheek.

She caught her breath, unsure which was more compelling, the look in his eyes or the stroke of his skin on hers. It seemed like ages since they'd touched...really touched. She ignored the quivering in her limbs and focused on his words.

"I need you to understand something. From now on, I plan on spending a lot of time with you and my girls. Together." Right there in the middle of the hospital corridor, he pulled her into his arms. "Is that all right with you?" he whispered.

She shivered then went hot all over at the sensual vibration of his lips against her ear. "Y-yes, it's okay with me," she managed.

"Good." He pulled back, but kept his arms around her waist. "So, is that a *yes* for dinner, too?"

She nodded despite the jittering dance of her stomach.

Chase looked at his watch. "Why don't you come over in an hour or so? I can't promise a gourmet meal, but I should be able come up with something palatable."

"Can I bring anything?"

"Just yourself." He kissed her again, and then he turned and headed toward the elevators. He winked at her before the doors closed, cutting off her view of him.

"Well, I guess he's not so much of an idiot after all."

Erika spun at the sound of Lauren's voice. "What?"

"I told him if he let you go he was a bigger idiot than my brother."

Erika's head whirled. She couldn't keep up with all of the revelations of the past hour. For the time being she ignored the part about Kevin. "When did you talk to Chase?"

Lauren shrugged. "One night when I picked the girls up."

Erika shook her head slowly from side to side. "I don't understand."

Lauren glanced around then gestured toward the empty couch in the waiting area. "Come, sit for a minute."

They sat. Lauren looked at Erika then away for a moment before meeting her gaze again. She huffed out a sigh. "Erika, I'm so sorry. About everything."

Erika didn't bother to try to hide her surprise. Lauren was apologizing to *her*?

Her sister-in-law gave a self-deprecating smile. "I know we haven't treated you very well lately. But I have to admit it came as a shock to find Chase at your house...the way I did." She held up a hand so Erika wouldn't interrupt. "I reacted badly, and then made things worse by telling Mom. But after I calmed down and had time to think about things in a rational way,

Jim made me realize you and Chase make a lot of sense together."

"He did?" Shock echoed in Erika's voice.

Lauren looked away and bit her lip. "Actually, he read me the riot act. He said I needed to let go of the past if he and I were ever going to have a future. He said I needed to make my relationship with my ex-husband work before I could move on with a new one. And he was right. I needed to let go of my anger toward Chase. So I did. Well, I'm working on it. Some days it's easier than others." She grimaced. "I've been angry with him for so long, it's more of a habit than anything else." Her laugh was wry and she shook her head. "I know it must sound strange to hear me say all of this."

"A little bit," Erika admitted. A lot bit. In fact, she'd be less surprised if Lauren sprouted wings and flew away right in front of her, but she didn't know what else to say. She chewed on a fingernail. Right now she couldn't analyze Lauren's comments too deeply. Not with her head still spinning. "What about Mom...Louise?" she blurted.

"I think she's coming around," Lauren said. "She loves you a lot, you know. Today I think she realized how much Chase means to you. This is hard on her. She still misses Kevin." She frowned. "And she doesn't know what he did to you."

Erika gasped. "Y-you knew?"

Lauren's lips pressed together. "I only figured it out right before he died." She glanced at Erika, her expression sharp. "How long had you known?"

"For a while," Erika admitted.

"Why didn't you tell anyone? Confront him? Or did you?"

Erika shook her head. "I was afraid."

"Afraid?" Now Lauren sounded surprised. "Of what?"

"Losing you. And Louise and Frank." She looked down at her hands twined in her lap. "I was afraid if you knew Kevin didn't love me anymore, you wouldn't either." She snuck a glance at Lauren.

Lauren's mouth opened and closed. "Oh, Erika." The words held a quiet anguish.

"You're the only real family I've ever had, and I couldn't imagine not being a part of it anymore. I didn't know what would happen to me if Kevin and I got divorced. I mean, I knew how you all felt about Chase after your divorce, even before then, and I knew I'd be the outsider if the same thing happened to me. I didn't think I could stand it if you hated me like that." The last came out almost in a whisper.

"It seems like I have more to apologize for than I thought. My situation with Chase isn't anything like your situation with Kevin."

"Wouldn't it have been? I mean, Kevin's your brother. He's Louise and Frank's son."

"But *he* cheated on *you*."

Erika winced. It still hurt after all this time to know she hadn't been good enough for her husband.

Lauren took her hand. "I really wish you would have told us."

"It was too humiliating. I mean, how do you explain to someone your husband doesn't think of you as the most important thing in his life?"

"Is that what you think?"

Erika grimaced. "It's the story of my life. Always second best. My mother left me. My father's wives

226

couldn't have cared less about me. Kevin cheated on me. Even Chase…" she faltered then took a deep breath. "And now, when I do have a family who cares about me, I go and try to ruin it with a man whose heart is so full of love for his children, there's no place for me." She held up her hand before Lauren could interrupt and shook her head ruefully. "Yikes, I sound pathetic. Look, I don't mean for this to be a pity party here. All I'm saying is there seems to be a pattern."

Lauren looked thoughtful for a moment. "I wish I could explain why all those things happened to you, but of course I can't. And since I don't have a psychology degree, take this with a grain of salt." She smiled. "But I'm going to go out on a limb here and say those people are the ones with issues, not you."

She squeezed Erika's fingers. "You are one of the most loving, loyal, giving, caring"—she made circles in the air with her other hand—"people I've ever met. So, for now, let's set aside your parents' and Kevin's issues. Even if we feel like strangling the bastards," she muttered under her breath. "And let's talk about Chase."

Erika gazed at Lauren warily. Where was she going with all of this?

Lauren inhaled, and then blew the breath out slowly. "The only reason Chase has issues is because of me."

Erika gaped. She rubbed her temples. She couldn't keep up.

Lauren gave a self-conscious laugh. "I know we've thrown a lot at you today, but I think you need to hear this, so if you'll bear with me for a moment or two longer?"

Erika nodded.

Lauren stared at the painting on the wall across from her, but Erika had the feeling she wasn't really seeing it. "You see my whole marriage to Chase was based on a lic." She glanced over at Erika. "Did you know I got pregnant on purpose?"

Erika stared then shook her head. She resisted the urge to grab it with both hands to make sure it didn't spin off of her shoulders.

"I was ready to get married. I mean, hell, all my friends were already married. My baby brother was married." She nodded toward Erika. "I wanted to be, too. Marriage didn't seem to be in Chase's plans, so I kind of forced his hand. And it worked. We got married. Exactly what I wanted. As you can imagine, he wasn't thrilled with the idea, but he really is a good guy, and he wanted to do the right thing. I figured he'd come around and everything would be okay. But it was harder than I thought, making it work. When the twins were born it got even harder. I wasn't ready to be a mom. I barely knew how to be a wife.

"Chase was a whole lot better at everything than I was. He really tried to be a good husband. Of course, fatherhood suited him right away. He seemed to like being a father more than he liked being a husband. Which I resented."

Erika frowned and took a moment to process what Lauren had said. Other than the truth about Lauren's pregnancy, nothing else was surprising. It only reinforced what she already knew. Chase's girls were everything to him.

Lauren must have caught the look on Erika's face. She shook her head. "Crap. I'm telling it wrong."

"What?"

"The point I'm trying to make is, when your whole relationship is based on a lie, how can it work?"

"Did Chase know? About you getting pregnant on purpose, I mean?"

"I never meant to tell him. It came out in the middle of one of our arguments. I guess you could say it was the straw that broke the camel's back. Things only got worse from there. Not long after that, we decided to separate."

Lauren fell silent for a moment. "Okay, I can see I'm still not telling it right. Here's the thing. Mom doesn't know any of this. So to her, he's always the bad guy. To Mom he's the guy who knocked up her little girl, and then gave up on his family. I did everything I could to encourage that idea. Someone had to take the blame, and I sure as hell didn't want it to be me, so that left him. It wasn't fair. We were both to blame. And if I'm being totally honest, the lion's share really should fall on me."

Erika shook her head to untangle the questions knotted up inside of it. After deliberating, she decided to ask outright. "Why are you telling me this now?"

Lauren smiled. "There are a couple of reasons. One is being in love with Jim." A blush stained her cheeks. "I understand what a real, committed relationship based on love and mutual respect is all about now. I'm able to look back and see all of the things I did wrong with Chase. Things I'm ashamed of."

"And two?" Erika prompted.

"Two, Chase makes you happy. Ever since you've been with him there's been something different about you. Something good."

Erika frowned. "But you didn't know about us."

"No, but I could tell something was up. You've been happier than I've seen you in a long time. And anyone who can make someone else as happy as he makes you, can't be all bad."

Erika sighed. "Other than sneaking around, I have been happy. But to be honest…" she hesitated. Talking to Lauren about her relationship with Chase was so strange, but at the same time, she needed to do it. "Chase and I went into this relationship knowing it couldn't last. I knew my family would never approve, and he wants nothing to do with getting married again." She looked over at Lauren. "Maybe I'm with Chase for all the wrong reasons, too."

Lauren shook her head. "No, you're not. Erika, I saw the way he looks at you. And the way you look at him. You're in love with each other…for all the right reasons."

"I don't know. So much has happened today I can't really wrap my head around it." She gestured as if to encompass the whole day. "And then Frank asked Chase if he was going to marry me." She put her head in her hands.

"What did Chase say?"

"He said he was," Erika mumbled through her fingers.

"See?" Lauren grinned. "Now we'll both get our happily ever afters."

Erika shook her head, unable to set aside the last bit of uncertainty. Could it really be that easy?

****

An hour later, Erika stood on Chase's doorstep. Her heart quivered. She wiped her sweaty palms on her shorts, and then took a deep gulp of air into her lungs. With trembling fingers, she pressed the doorbell.

The door flung open to reveal two excited faces grinning up at her. "Hi, Aunt Erika!"

"You're having dinner at our house." Sami clapped her hands.

Erika knelt and wrapped her arms around both girls.

Chase appeared in the doorway from the kitchen. His gaze met hers. A deep satisfaction lit his dark eyes. "Hi," he said.

She rose. "Hi, yourself." With the girls looking on she quelled the instinct to run into his arms and demand he carry her to the bedroom.

An answering flicker of restraint glimmered in his eyes. "Dinner's almost ready."

"Let's read a book 'til it's done." Steph grabbed Erika's hand.

"No, let's set the table like I asked you to." Chase sent his daughter a meaningful look.

"Rats."

Erika laughed.

"C'mon." Sami tugged on her arm. "You can help." In the kitchen, she pointed to the cabinet next to the refrigerator. "The dishes are up there. We're big enough to put them on the table but not big enough to get them down. Daddy usually does it, but you can now since you're here today too."

Erika retrieved the plates from the cabinet and set them on the table. With intense concentration, Sami distributed them to the right places. Meanwhile, Steph got silverware out of a drawer and carefully added a fork to each setting.

"Don't forget the napkins," Chase said over his shoulder from his position at the stove.

"I'll get them."

"No, I will."

The girls pushed at each other on their way to the counter.

"You can both get them." Chase looked over at Erika and shook his head. "Sorry, they're a little overexcited."

"I don't mind."

"I hope you're okay with Pasta a la Sami and Steph."

"Pasta a la Sami and Steph?"

"Pasta mixed with tomato soup and cut up hotdogs thrown in for good measure," Chase explained.

"It's our favorite," Steph piped up.

"Yeah, Daddy makes it special, just for us," Sami added.

"Well, then I'm sure I'll love it," Erika assured them.

Steph came over and settled herself against Erika's knees, while Sami wandered over to hug Chase's legs.

"Is it done yet, Daddy? I'm starving."

Erika laughed at the drama dripping from the little girl's voice, and Chase ruffled her hair with his free hand. "Oh, I'm sure you are. Did you put cups out for milk?"

"Nope. Can't reach." Sami shrugged.

"I'll get them." Erika handed the cups to the girls who added them to the table.

Steph surveyed it with fists on her hips. "Okay. It's all done. Are we gonna eat or what?"

"Go wash your hands. When you get back, dinner

will be ready." As soon as the girls left the room, Chase pulled Erika up from her chair and kissed her. She wrapped her arms around his neck and melted into him. "I've been wanting to do that since you got here." He nuzzled her nose with his.

"It was worth the wait."

"Oh, but you haven't seen anything yet. Wait until later." He kissed her one last time before he turned his attention back to dinner. He filled each plate with the pasta concoction, and when the girls returned they all sat down.

"Hands," Steph instructed and held hers toward Erika on one side and Chase on the other.

"This is how we say the prayers," Sami explained as she took Erika's other hand.

They all bowed their heads and murmured thanks over the food.

"Okay, dig in," Chase said.

"Finally."

****

Later, after stories had been read, prayers heard, and both girls were tucked into bed, Chase made good on his promise of more things to come. When his kisses had rendered her nearly senseless, Erika found enough strength to push him away.

"Not with the girls right down the hall," she explained after catching her breath.

He nodded. "I know. I wouldn't have taken it much further tonight." He smeared his thumb over her bottom lip. "But I missed you."

"I missed you, too." She combed her fingers through the hair falling over his forehead.

"It's something you'll need to get used to, you

know. Making love with me while the girls are right down the hall. We'll both have to get used to it."

"True, but I'm thinking a locked bedroom door and not the couch in the wide open living room is the way to go."

"Probably a wise decision." He toyed with a lock of her hair. "Thanks for coming to dinner tonight."

"You're welcome. I had fun."

"Did you?"

She frowned. "Of course. Why would you even ask?"

"The girls' exuberance can be a lot to take sometimes."

"They're five, Chase, I wouldn't expect anything else."

He framed her face in his hands and kissed her tenderly. "I love you, Erika. You know that, right?"

Her heart turned to goo. She touched the side of his face. "I do now." Her fingers feathered over his lips. "I love you, too." The relief and joy to finally say the words out loud made her almost dizzy with giddiness.

"Good." He took her hand in his and studied their twined fingers. "I wasn't placating Frank at the hospital earlier. I want to marry you." His gaze captured hers with a soft intensity.

Her gooshy heart fluttered. Joy filled her, however she heard the unspoken end of his sentence. She voiced it out loud. "But?"

He offered a smile and raised her fingers to his lips for a kiss. "You really do know me well if you can read my mind." He ran his thumb over her neon orange fingernails. "But, I wonder if you really want to marry me."

Her jaw dropped. "Why wouldn't I?"

He looked at her, letting his gaze linger on hers for long, delicious moments. "Because marrying me is kind of a package deal. You wouldn't be marrying only me. The girls would be part of it, too."

She frowned. "Of course they would. I love Sami and Steph."

"I know you do. You're the best aunt in the world. But being a stepmom is different."

"Yes, it would be different."

"You know, most of the time, a man and woman get married and have some time to get used to each other as a couple. Alone. It wouldn't be like that for us. At least not all the time. The girls come every weekend."

"I know. I really do enjoy spending time with them."

"And," he hesitated. "I'd want to give them some time to get used to you as more than Aunt Erika."

"I think that's a good idea."

His grip on her hand tightened. "Believe me, if it was only me, I'd marry you tomorrow." His voice sounded almost desperate. "But I have to think about my girls, too."

Erika fell in love with him all over again. She shifted to kneel on the couch next to him. She took his face in her hands and kissed him. "Of course you do. The way you are with the twins is one of the things I love the most about you. I wouldn't want you to do anything that wasn't right for them."

"I don't love them more than you. I love them differently than I love you."

"I know." And she did. Chase could love her and

235

the girls. Neither would be first or second. They'd all have a place in his heart.

"What about the family?"

"What about them?"

"They seem to be taking things—us—fairly well. Surprisingly well. At least Lauren and Frank are. What about Louise? Can she accept me in your life?"

"I think she will eventually." She hesitated. "Things may be tense for a little while."

"You're okay with that?"

"It won't be easy, but Chase, you belong in my life. Everything else will work itself out." With him by her side, she'd face whatever came her way. No more secrets and no more lies.

"And you're really okay waiting to get married for a little while? It won't be long. And then I promise, it will be forever."

She wiggled onto his lap and snuggled into him. She'd waited a long time to hear those words from him. It wouldn't kill her to wait a little longer. The promise in his eyes reassured her. Soon her life would change. Not in the devastating, horrible way it had a few weeks ago, but in a wonderful, amazing, unforgettable way.

"Yep, I'm okay with it."

Chapter Sixteen

A year later to the day, Erika stood in the living room of her completely renovated row house waiting for the ceremony to begin.

They'd decided against a formal church wedding, instead opting to say their vows in the home they'd created together. The physical labor had been a big part of it, but more so it was the place their love had truly begun.

Chase would officially move in after their honeymoon, although he already spent most of the week there. One of the bedrooms upstairs had been decorated with a mermaid theme for the twins on weekends.

The girls would be the only attendants as Erika and Chase exchanged vows in front of a small group of friends and family gathered in the backyard.

Chase had invited his parents and sister, but Erika had kept her guest list to a few close friends from school. She'd let her father and his current wife know she was getting married, but hadn't invited them to the event. The same went for Louise and Frank. Frank's easy acceptance of her relationship with Chase had helped Louise come to terms with it far quicker than Erika ever imagined, but Louise still mourned for Kevin and Erika hadn't wanted to pour salt in the wound by extending an invitation.

Erika had talked to Lauren about coming, but Lauren had joked and said it was probably in bad taste to invite the groom's ex-wife to witness the beginning of his new marriage.

She checked her reflection in the mirror in the entryway one final time. Flowers wove through the simple twist of curls atop her head. A strapless ivory sheath curved over her hips. Strappy sandals with a thin heel peeked out from beneath the slightly flared, floor-length hem.

"You look beautiful."

Erika turned at the sound of Chase's voice. Since theirs had been far from a traditional romance in the first place, they hadn't worried about any of the nonsense of not seeing the bride before the wedding.

Her gaze slid over his formal black suit with a champagne colored shirt and tie beneath. "You don't look so bad yourself."

He grinned and her heart skipped in its steady rhythm. But when he lowered his head, she placed a hand on his chest. "You'll ruin my make-up."

His sigh fanned warm breath over her face. "Right. I guess the groom really shouldn't wear lipstick to the wedding." He rubbed his nose across hers.

She laughed. "Exactly."

Before she could say anything else, like how much she loved him and adored him and couldn't wait for him to kiss all of her lipstick off later, Sami and Steph raced into the room.

Sami skidded to a stop in front of Chase. "When's the wedding gonna start?"

Chase looked at his watch. "Soon."

Steph sidled over to Erika. "You look like a

princess, Aunt Erika."

"Then you two must be my beautiful ladies-in-waiting."

"We have fancy dresses, too. See?" Steph whirled to make the bell of her ivory sundress flare out.

"Me too, me too." Sami copied her sister.

"Okay. Enough spinning." Chase steadied them. "We don't want dizzy flower girls."

"Rats." Steph pouted for two seconds. "Did you see our hairdos?" She pointed to the crown of flowers twisted around her head.

"Very fancy," Erika said.

"Daddy braided our hair and then put on the flowers. But not all of our hair, just a little bit. The rest has curls like yours."

Teri walked in from the kitchen and handed Erika a bouquet of calla lilies. She glanced at Chase. "Everyone's here. Let's get you two married."

Chase's gaze met Erika's. A spark lit the dark mocha of his irises. "Sounds good to me." He held out his hand.

She slipped hers into his warm grasp. "Me too."

"Daddy's gonna marry Aunt Erika," Sami said to Teri.

"Well then we'd better get your baskets. There can't be a wedding unless the flower girls have their flowers."

The girls danced in front of Erika and Chase into the kitchen. Teri handed them each a wicker basket overflowing with miniature ivory and peach roses. She looked at Erika. "Give me a minute to cue the music." She disappeared out the French doors leading to the patio.

Chase squeezed Erika's hand. The warmth and love of his touch flowed through her. "You ready?"

"Absolutely. You?"

"I've never been more ready for anything in my life." He raised her hand to his lips and brushed a kiss across the knuckles. The warm tingle spread, sinking deeper into her soul. "I love you."

"I love you too."

From outside, the first strains of *Jesu, Joy of Man's Desiring*, played by a duet of violin and cello, filtered into the house.

"That's our cue." Chase guided the twins into position. "Sami and Steph, you go first. We'll follow you. Just like we practiced."

The girls linked hands and pranced through the open doors. Erika tucked her hand into the crook of Chase's elbow. The music wrapped around her, joining with the joy in her heart and filling her soul with the wonder of the moment and of loving Chase and being loved in return. Nothing in her entire life had ever been so perfect.

She stepped out onto the patio. The dozen or so guests gathered in the small space turned to face them. After another step she froze when her gaze fell on two of the faces near the cobblestone path leading around the side of the house.

Frank offered a wide smile. And while Louise's was a little more restrained, she smiled as well.

Erika looked up at Chase, whose lips curved too. "You knew they were coming?"

He nodded. "They wanted to surprise you."

Tears pricked her eyes. She swallowed. How was it possible? The perfect moment had gotten even better.

Sweeter.

Chase tugged gently on her arm. They resumed their slow walk to the preacher waiting beneath an arbor at the edge of the patio. Intertwined calla lilies and peach roses decorated the white wooden structure. Later it would be moved to the side garden to become a permanent feature of the landscape. And a reminder of this day.

Not that she'd need it. Every minute detail from the musical notes flowing around her to the firm muscle of Chase's arm beneath her fingers to the smell of the gardenias in the yard would be etched in her memory forever.

Erika handed her bouquet to Sami and then turned to face Chase. The summer sun shining down on her couldn't compete with the warmth of her hands in his. As always, his strength burned into her, chasing away any shadows lurking in her soul.

"Friends and family." The preacher looked out at the guests. "We are gathered here today to join Chase and Erika in holy matrimony. It is indeed a special day when hearts joined by love will now be joined by name and life as well.

"Erika, do you take Chase to be your lawfully wedded husband? To have and to hold from this day forward, in sickness and in and health, and forsaking all others until death parts you?"

"I do."

"Chase, do you take Erika..." The words faded as she lost herself in the dark eyes of the man staring at her with so much love in them, she could almost feel its weight wrap around her. Instead of the preacher's voice, she heard Chase's soul speaking to hers as he vowed to love her forever.

"I do." The words echoed the silent promise in his eyes.

"May I have the rings?"

Sami and Steph each placed a satin bag tied with a ribbon on the top into the minister's outstretched hand. Their faces wore identical expressions of solemn concentration.

After blessing the rings, he held the smaller of the two out to Chase.

Chase took it and slid it partway onto Erika's finger. "With this ring, I thee wed." He pushed it into place then raised her hand to brush a kiss across it. The whisper of his touch shivered through her.

Erika placed the remaining ring on Chase's finger and repeated the pledge.

"Let us pray."

The guests bowed their heads, but unable to take her gaze from Chase, Erika didn't join in the respectful gesture. She hoped God didn't mind.

"Lord, bless Erika and Chase as they begin their life together. Guide and protect them on the road they travel, and surround them with the love of family and friends. Watch over their marriage and the family they become today."

Erika took Steph's hand, and Chase took Sami's.

"As not only two, but four hearts are joined in love. Amen.

"Erika. Chase. I now pronounce you husband and wife. You may kiss the bride."

Chase's eyes sparkled. With his free hand, he cupped the side of her face. The slightly rough pad of his thumb brushed her cheek. His lips met hers in a sweet, warm, and all-too-brief kiss.

Then he smiled at her, and the sunshine grew brighter, hotter, as their love took wings and joined its energizing force.

"Yay!" Sami clapped her hands.

"Daddy married Aunt Erika!" Steph chimed in.

Chase kissed Erika again then drew her and the girls into his arms for a hug as the guests burst into applause.

"I swear to you, Erika," he whispered for only her to hear. "I'll spend the rest of my life making sure your dreams always come true."

She pulled back to brush a strand of dark hair off his forehead and smiled despite the moisture stinging her eyes. "You won't have to work very hard. With you in my life, I don't have to dream. I have everything I've always wanted."

A word about the author...

Debra St. John has been reading and writing romance since high school. She always dreamed about publishing a romance novel some day. Her dream came true when she started writing sultry contemporary romance with sexy heroes and spunky heroines for The Wild Rose Press. Although she's a country gal at heart, she lives in a suburb of Chicago with her husband, who is her real-life hero.

She is the author of The Corral Series, which includes her debut release, *This Time for Always*, a Champagne Rose and Rosebud bestseller at The Wild Rose Press. The second book in the series, *This Can't Be Love*, was the Best of 2010 Contemporary Winner at Love Romances Cafe. *This Feels Like Home* completes the series.

Her holiday stories include *A Christmas to Remember*, *An Unexpected Blessing* (Thanksgiving), and *The Vampire and the Vixen* for Halloween.

Family Secrets and *Wild Wedding Weekend* complete her current bookshelf.

You can find her at:

www.debrastjohnromance.com
http://heroineswithhearts.blogspot.com
http://bookbeatbabes.blogspot.com
www.authorsbymoonlight.com

www.ingramcontent.com/pod-product-compliance
Lightning Source LLC
Chambersburg PA
CBHW070051260626
47160CB00004B/1169